D0503345

JACK KEROUAC

LONESOME TRAVELER

**DRAWINGS BY
LARRY RIVERS**

McGraw-Hill Book Company, Inc.
New York   Toronto   London

LONESOME TRAVELER

Portions of this book have appeared in
Holiday, The Evergreen Review, Jubilee,
and *Escapade.* Lines from *The Buddhist
Bible,* edited by Dwight Goddard, are
reproduced by permission of E. P. Dutton &
Co., Inc.

First Edition

34195

BOOKS BY JACK KEROUAC
The Town and the City
On the Road
The Dharma Bums
The Subterraneans
Dr. Sax
Maggie Cassidy
Visions of Cody
Tristessa
Lonesome Traveler

POETRY
Mexico City Blues

CONTENTS

Piers of the Homeless Night   1

Mexico Fellaheen   21

The Railroad Earth   37

Slobs of the Kitchen Sea   84

New York Scenes   104

Alone on a Mountaintop   118

Big Trip to Europe   135

The Vanishing American Hobo   172

NAME   Jack Kerouac

NATIONALITY   Franco-American

PLACE OF BIRTH   Lowell, Massachusetts

DATE OF BIRTH   March 12, 1922

EDUCATION   (*schools attended, special courses of study, degrees and years*)
Lowell (Mass.) High School; Horace Mann School for Boys; Columbia College (1940–42); New School for Social Research (1948–49). Liberal arts, no degrees (1936–1949). Got an A from Mark Van Doren in English at Columbia (Shakespeare course).—— Flunked chemistry at Columbia.—— Had a 92 average at Horace Mann School (1939–40). Played football on varsities. Also track, baseball, chess teams.

MARRIED   Nah

CHILDREN   No

SUMMARY OF PRINCIPAL OCCUPATIONS AND/OR JOBS
Everything: Let's elucidate: scullion on ships, gas station attendant, deckhand on ships, newspaper sportswriter (*Lowell Sun*), railroad brakeman, script synopsizer for 20th Century Fox in N.Y., soda jerk, railroad yardclerk, also railroad baggagehandler, cottonpicker, assistant furniture mover, sheet metal apprentice on the Pentagon in 1942, forest service fire lookout 1956, construction laborer (1941).

INTERESTS

HOBBIES   I invented my own baseball game, on cards, extremely complicated, and am in the process of playing a whole 154-game season among eight clubs, with all the works, batting averages, E.R.A. averages, etc.

SPORTS   Played all of them except tennis and lacrosse and skull.

SPECIAL   Girls

PLEASE GIVE A BRIEF RESUME OF YOUR LIFE
Had beautiful childhood, my father a printer in Lowell, Mass.,

roamed fields and riverbanks day and night, wrote little novels in my room, first novel written at age 11, also kept extensive diaries and "newspapers" covering my own-invented horseracing and baseball and football worlds (as recorded in novel *Doctor Sax*). —— Had good early education from Jesuit brothers at St. Joseph's Parochial School in Lowell making me jump sixth grade in public school later on; as child traveled to Montreal, Quebec, with family; was given a horse at age 11 by mayor of Lawrence (Mass.), Billy White, gave rides to all kids in neighborhood; horse ran away. Took long walks under old trees of New England at night with my mother and aunt. Listened to their gossip attentively. Decided to become a writer at age 17 under influence of Sebastian Sampas, local young poet who later died on Anzio beach head; read the life of Jack London at 18 and decided to also be an adventurer, a lonesome traveler; early literary influences Saroyan and Hemingway; later Wolfe (after I had broken leg in Freshman football at Columbia read Tom Wolfe and roamed his New York on crutches).—— Influenced by older brother Gerard Kerouac who died at age 9 in 1926 when I was 4, was great painter and drawer in childhood (he was) —— (also said to be a saint by the nuns) —— (recorded in forthcoming novel *Visions of Gerard*).—— My father was completely honest man full of gaiety; soured in last years over Roosevelt and World War II and died of cancer of the spleen.—— Mother still living, I live with her a kind of monastic life that has enabled me to write as much as I did.—— But also wrote on the road, as hobo, railroader, Mexican exile, Europe travel (as shown in *Lonesome Traveler*).—— One sister, Caroline, now married to Paul E. Blake Jr. of Henderson N.C., a government anti-missile technician —— she has one son, Paul Jr., my nephew, who calls me Uncle Jack and loves me.—— My mother's name Gabrielle, learned all about natural story-telling from her long stories about Montreal and New Hampshire.—— My people go back to Breton France, first North American ancestor Baron Alexandre Louis Lebris de Kérouac of Cornwall, Brittany, 1750 or so, was granted land along the Rivière du Loup after victory of Wolfe over Montcalm; his descendents married Indians (Mohawk and Caughnawaga) and became potato farmers; first United States descendant my grandfather Jean-Baptiste Kérouac, carpenter, Nashua N.H.—— My father's mother a Bernier related to explorer Bernier —— all Bretons on father's side —— My mother has a Norman name, L'Evesque.——

First formal novel *The Town and the City* written in tradition of long work and revision, from 1946 to 1948, three years, published by Harcourt Brace in 1950.—— Then discovered "spontaneous" prose and wrote, say, *The Subterraneans* in 3 nights —— wrote *On the Road* in 3 weeks ——

Read and studied alone all my life.—— Set a record at Columbia College cutting classes in order to stay in dormitory room to write a daily play and read, say, Louis Ferdinand Céline, instead of "classics" of the course.——

Had own mind.—— Am known as "madman bum and angel" with "naked endless head" of "prose."—— Also a verse poet, *Mexico City Blues* (Grove, 1959).—— Always considered writing my duty on earth. Also the preachment of universal kindness, which hysterical critics have failed to notice beneath frenetic activity of my true-story novels about the "beat" generation.—— Am actually not "beat" but strange solitary crazy Catholic mystic . . .

Final plans: hermitage in the woods, quiet writing of old age, mellow hopes of Paradise (which comes to everybody anyway) . . .

Favorite complaint about contemporary world: the facetiousness of "respectable" people . . . who, because not taking anything seriously, are destroying old human feelings older than *Time Magazine* . . . Dave Garroways laughing at white doves . . .

PLEASE GIVE A SHORT DESCRIPTION OF THE BOOK, ITS SCOPE AND PURPOSE AS YOU SEE THEM

Lonesome Traveler is a collection of published and unpublished pieces connected together because they have a common theme: Traveling.

The travels cover the United States from the south to the east coast to the west coast to the far northwest, cover Mexico, Morocco Africa, Paris, London, both the Atlantic and Pacific oceans at sea in ships, and various interesting people and cities therein included.

Railroad work, sea work, mysticism, mountain work, lasciviousness, solepsism, self-indulgence, bullfights, drugs, churches, art museums, streets of cities, a mishmosh of life as lived by an independent educated penniless rake going anywhere.

Its scope and purpose is simply poetry, or, natural description.

vi

1. PIERS OF THE HOMELESS NIGHT

HERE DOWN ON DARK EARTH
    before we all go to Heaven
VISIONS OF AMERICA
All that hitchhikin
All that railroadin
All that comin back
    to America
Via Mexican & Canadian borders . . .
    Less begin with the sight of me with collar huddled
up close to neck and tied around with a handkerchief to
keep it tight and snug, as I go trudging across the bleak,
dark warehouse lots of the ever lovin San Pedro waterfront, the oil refineries smelling in the damp foggish
night of Christmas 1951 just like burning rubber and
the brought-up mysteries of Sea Hag Pacific, where just
off to my left as I trudge you can see the oily skeel of
old bay waters marching up to hug the scummy posts
and out on over the flatiron waters are the lights ululat-

ing in the moving tide and also lights of ships and bum boats themselves moving and closing in and leaving this last lip of American land.—— Out on that dark ocean, that wild dark sea, where the worm invisibly rides to come, like a hag flying and laid out as if casually on sad sofa but her hair flying and she's on her way to find the crimson joy of lovers and eat it up, Death by name, the doom and death ship the S.S. *Roamer*, painted black with orange booms, was coming now like a ghost and without a sound except for its vastly shuddering engine, to be warped & wailed in at the Pedro pier, fresh from a run from New York through the Panamy canal, and aboard's my ole buddy Deni Bleu let's call him who had me travel 3,000 miles overland on buses with the promise he will get me on and I sail the rest of the trip around the world.—— And since I'm well and on the bum again & aint got nothing else to do, but roam, long-faced, the real America, with my unreal heart, here I am eager and ready to be a big busted nose scullion or dish-washer on the old scoff scow s'long as I can buy my next fancy shirt in a Hong Kong haberdashery or wave a polo mallet in some old Singapore bar or play the horses in Australian, it's all the same to me as long as it can be exciting and goes around the world.

For weeks I have been traveling on the road, west from New York, and waiting up in Frisco at a friend's house meanwhile earning an extra 50 bucks working the Christmas rush as a baggagehandler with the old sop out railroad, have just now come the 500 miles down from Frisco as an honored secret guest in the caboose of the Zipper first class freight train thanx to my con-nections on the railroad up there and now I think I'm going to be a big seaman, I'll get on the *Roamer* right here in Pedro, so I think fondly, anyway if it wasnt for this shipping I'd sure like it maybe to be a railroad man, learn to be a brakeman, and get paid to ride that old zooming Zipper.—— But I'd been sick, a sudden choking awful cold of the virus X type California style, and could hardly see out the dusty window of the caboose as it flashed past the snowy breaking surf at Surf and Tangair and Gaviota on the division that runs that moony rail between San Luis Obispo and Santa Barbara.—— I'd tried my best to appreciate a good ride but could only lay flat on the caboose seat with my face buried in my bundled jacket and every conductor from San Jose to Los Angeles had had to wake me up to ask about my qualifications, I was a brakeman's brother and a brakeman in Texas Division myself, so whenever I looked up thinking "Ole Jack you are now actually riding in a caboose and going along the surf on the spectrallest railroad you'd ever in your wildest little dreams wanta ride, like a kid's dream, why is it you cant lift your head and look out there and appreciate the feathery shore of California the last land being feathered by fine powdery skeel of doorstop sills of doorstep water weaving in from every Orient and bay boom shroud from here to Catteras Flapperas Voldivious and Gratteras, boy," but I'd raise my head, and nothing there was to see, except my bloodshot soul, and vague hints of an unreal moon shinin on an unreal sea, and the flashby quick of the pebbles of the road bed, the rail in the starlight.—— Arriving in L.A. in the morning and I stagger with full huge cuddlebag on shoulder from the L.A. yards clear into downtown Main Street L.A. where I laid up in a hotel room 24 hours drinking bourbon lemon juice and anacin and seeing as I lay on my back a vision of America that had no end —— which was only beginning —— thinking, tho, "I'll get on the *Roamer* at Pedro and be gone for Japan before you can say boo."—— Looking out the window when I felt a little better and digging the hot sunny streets of L.A. Christmas, going down finally to the skid row poolhalls and shoe shine

3

joints and gouging around, waiting for the time when the *Roamer* would warp in at the Pedro pier, where I was to meet Deni right at the gangplank with the gun he'd sent ahead.

More reasons than one for the meeting in Pedro —— he'd sent a gun ahead inside of a book which he'd carefully cut and hollowed out and made into a tight neat package covered with brown paper and tied with string, addressed to a girl in Hollywood, Helen something, with address which he gave me, "Now Kerouac when you get to Hollywood you go immediately to Helen's and ask her for that package I sent her, then you carefully open it in your hotel room and there's the gun and it's loaded so be careful dont shoot your finger off, then you put it in your pocket, do you hear me Kerouac, has it gotten into your heskefuffle frantic imagination —— but now you've got a little errand to do for me, for your boy Denny Blue, remember we went to school together, we thought up ways to survive together to scrounge for pennies we were even cops together we even married the same woman," (cough) "I mean,—— we both wanted the same woman, Kerouac, it's up to you now now to help defend me against the evil of Matthew Peters, you bring that gun with you" poking me and emphatically pronouncing each word and poking me with each word "and bring it on you and dont get caught and dont miss the boat whatever you do."—A plan so absurd, so typical of this maniac, I came of course without the gun, without even looking up Helen, but just in my beatup jacket hurrying, almost late, I could see her masts close in against the pier, night, spotlights everywhere, down that dismal long plaza of refineries and oil storage tanks, on my poor scuffledown shoes that had begun a real journey now —— starting in New York to follow the fool ship but it was about to be made plain to me in the first 24 hours I'd never get on no ship ——

4

didnt know it then, but was doomed to stay in America, always, road rail or waterscrew, it'll always be America (Orient-bound ships chugging up the Mississippi, as will be shown later.)—No gun, huddled against the awful winter damp of Pedro and Long Beach, in the night, passing the Puss n' Boots factory on a corner with little lawn out front and American flagpoles and a big tuna fish ad inside the same building they make fish for humans and for cats —— passing the Matson piers, the Lurline not in.—— Eyes peeled for Matthew Peters the villain who was behind the need for the gun.

It went back, maniacally, to further earlier events in this gnashing huge movie of earth only a piece of which here's offered by me, long tho it is, how wild can the world be until finally you realize "O well it's just repetitious anyway."—— But Deni had deliberately wrecked this Matthew Peters' car. It seems they had lived together and with a bunch of girls in Hollywood. They were seamen. You saw snapshots of them sitting around sunny pools in bathingsuits and with blondes and in big hugging poses. Deni tall, fattish, dark, smiling white teeth hypocrite's smile, Matthew Peters an extremely handsome blond with a self-assured grim expression or (morbid) expression of sin and silence, the hero —— of the group, of the time —— so that you hear it always spoken behind the hand, the confidential stories told to you by every drunk and non-drunk in every bar and non-bar from here to the other side of all the Tathagata worlds in the 10 Quarters of the universe, it's like the ghosts of all the mosquitos that had ever lived, the density of the story of the world all of it would be enough to drown the Pacific as many times as you could remove a grain of sand from its sandy bed. The big story was, the big complaint, that I heard chanted, from Deni, an old complainer and chanter and one of the most vituperative of complainers, "While I was scroung-

ing around in the garbage cans and barrels of Hollywood mind you, going behind those very fancy apartment houses and at night, late, very quietly sneaking
around, getting bottles for 5 cent deposits and putting
them in my little bag, for extra money, when we
couldnt get longshore work and nor get a ship for love
nor money, Matthew, with his airy ways, was having
big parties and spending every cent he could get from
my grimy hands and not once, N O TTT Once, did I
hear one W O R D of appreciation —— you can imagine
how I felt when finally he took my best girl and took
off with her for a night —— I sneaked to his garage
where he had his car parked, I very quietly backed it
out without starting the motor, I let it roll down the
street, and then man I was on my way to Frisco, drinking beer from cans —— I could tell you a story ——"
and so he goes on with his story, told in his own inimit-
able way, how he wrecked the car in Cucamonga California, a head-on crash into some tree, how he almost
got killed, how the cops were, and lawyers, and papers,
and troubles, and how he finally got to Frisco, and got
another ship, and how Matthew Peters who knew he
was on the *Roamer*, would be waiting at the pierhead
this very same clammy cold night in Pedro with a gun,
a knife, henchmen, friends, anything and everything.——
Deni was going to step off the ship looking in all directions, ready to throw himself flat on the ground, and
I was to be waiting there at the foot of the gangplank
and hand him the gun real quick —— all in the foggy
foggy night ——

"Alright tell me a story."

"Gently now."

"Well you're the one who started all this."

"Gently, gently" says Deni in his own peculiar way
saying "JHENT" very loud with mouth moawed like
a radio announcer to pronounce every sound and then

the "LY" is just said English-wise, it was a trick we'd both picked up at a certain madcap prep school where everybody went around talking like very high smotche smahz, ... now shmuz, SHmazaa zzz, inexplicable the foolish tricks of schoolboys long ago, lost,—— which Deni now in the absurd San Pedro night was still quipping up to fogs, as if it didnt make any difference.—— "GENT ly" says Deni taking a firm grip on my arm and holding me tight and looking at me seriously, he's about six-three and he's looking down at little five-nine me and his eyes are dark, glittering, you can see he's mad, you can see his conception of life is something no one else has ever had and ever will have tho just as seriously he can go around believing and claiming his theory about me for instance, "Kerouac is a victim, a VIC timm of his own i ma JHI NA Tion."—— Or his favorite joke about me, which is supposed to be so funny and is the saddest story he ever told or anyone ever told, "Kerouac wouldnt accept a leg of fried chicken one night and when I asked him why he said 'I'm thinking about the poor starving people of Europe'... Hyaa WA W W W" and he goes off on his fantastic laugh which is a great shrieking lofter into a sky designed specially for him and which I always see over him when I think of him, the black night, the around the world night, the night he stood on the pier in Honolulu with contraband Japanese kimonos on, four of them, and the customs guards made him undress down to em and there he stands at night on the platform in Japanese kimonos, big huge Deni Bleu, downcast & very very unhappy —— "I could tell you a story that's so long I couldnt finish telling it to you if we took a trip around the world, Kerouac, you but you dont you wont you never liste —— Kerouac what WHAT are you going to tell the poor people starving in Europe about the Puss n' Boots plant there with the tuna fish in back, H MHmmh Ya

7

aYYaawww Yawww, *they make the same food for cats and people,* Yyorr yhOOOOOOOOOO!"——And when he laughed like that you know he was having a hell of a good time and lonely in it, because I never saw it to fail, the fellas on the ship and all ships he ever sailed on couldnt see what was so funny what with all, also, his practical joking, which I'll show.—— "I wrecked Matthew Peters' car you understand—— now let me say of course I didnt do it deliberately, Matthew Peters would like to think so, a lot of evil skulls like to believe so, Paul Lyman likes to believe so so he can also believe I stole his wife which I assure you Kerouac I ding e do, it was my buddy Harry McKinley who stole Paul Lyman's wife—— I drove Matthew's car to Frisco, I was going to leave it there on the street and ship out, he would have got the thing back but unfortunately, Kerouac, life isnt always outcome could coming the way we like and tie but the name of the town I can never and I shall never be able to—— there, up, er, Kerouac, you're not listening," gripping my arm "Gently now, are you listening to what I'm SAYING to you!"

"Of course I'm listening."

"Then why are you going myu, m, hu, what's up there, the birds up there, you heard the bird up there, mmmmy" turning away with a little shnuffle lonely laugh, this is when I see the true Deni, now, when he turns away, it isnt a big joke, there was no way to make it a big joke, he was talking to me and then he tried to make a joke out of my seeming not-listening and it wasnt funny because I was listening, in fact I was seriously listening as always to all his complaints and songs and but he turned away and had tried and in a forlorn little look into his own, as if, past, you see the double chin or dimplechin of some big baby nature folding up and with rue, with a heartbreaking, French giving-up, humility, meekness even, he ran the gamut from abso-

lutely malicious plotting and scheming and practical joking, to big angel Ananda baby mourning in the night, I saw him I know.—— "Cucamonga, Practamonga, Calamongonata, I shall shall never remember the name of that town, but I ran the car head-on into a tree, Jack, and that was that and I was set upon by every scroungy cop lawyer judge doctor indian chief insurance salesman conman type in the —— I tell you I was lucky to get away alive I had to wire home for all kinds of money, as you know my mother in Vermont has all my savings and when I'm in a real pinch I always wire home, it's my money."

"Yes Deni." But to cap everything there was Matthew Peters' buddy Paul Lyman, who had a wife, who ran away with Harry McKinley or in some way that I could never understand, they took a lot of money and got on an Orient bound passenger vessel and were now living with an alcoholic major in a villa in Singapore and having a big time in white duck trousers and tennis shoes but Lyman the husband, also a seaman and in fact a shipmate of Matthew Peters' and (tho Den didn't know at this time, aboard the Lurline both of them) (keep that) bang, he was convinced Deni was behind that too, and so the both of them had sworn to kill Deni or get Deni and according to Deni they were going to be on the pier when the ship came in that night, with guns and friends, and I was to be there, ready, when Deni comes off the gangplank swiftly and all dressed up to go to Hollywood to see his stars and girls and all the big things he'd written me I'm to step up quickly and hand him the gun, loaded and cocked, and Deni, looking around carefully to see no shadows leap up, ready to throw himself flat on the ground, takes the gun from me and together we cut into the darkness of the waterfront and rush to town —— for further events, developments ——

9

So now the *Roamer* was coming in, it was being straightened out along the concrete pier, I stood and spoke quietly to one of the after deckhands struggling with ropes, "Where's the carpenter?"

"Who Blue? the —— I'll see him in a minute." A few other requests and out comes Deni just as the ship is being winched and secured and the ordinary's putting out the rat guards and the captain's blowed his little whistle and that incomprehensible slow huge slowmotion eternity move of ships is done, you hear the churns the backwater churns, the pissing of scuppers —— the big ghostly trip is done, the ship is in —— the same human faces are on the deck —— and here comes Deni in his dungarees and unbelievably in the foggy night he sees his boy standing right there on the quai, just as planned, with hands-a-pockets, almost could reach out and touch him.

"There you are Kerouac, I never thought you'd be here."

"You told me to, didnt you ——"

"Wait, another half hour to finish up and clean up and dress, I'll be right with you —— anybody around?"

"I dont know." I looked around. I had been looking around for a half hour, at parked cars, dark corners, holes of sheds, door holes, niches, crypts of Egypt, waterfront rat holes, crapule doorholes, and beercan clouts, midmast booms and fishing eagles —— bah, nowhere, the heroes were nowhere to be seen.

TWO OF THE SADDEST DOGS you ever saw (haw haw haw) walking off that pier, in the dark, past a few customs guards who gave Deni a customary little look and wouldnt have found the gun in his pocket anyway but he'd taken all those pains to mail it in that hollowed-out tome and now as we peered around together he whispered "Well have you got it?"

"Yea yea in my pocket."

"Hang on to it, give to me outside on the street."

"Dont worry."

"I guess they're not here, but you never can tell."

"I looked everywhere."

"We'll get outa here and make tracks —— I've got it all planned Kerouac what we're gonna do tonight tomorrow and the whole weekend; I've been talking to all the cooks, we've got it all planned, a letter for you down to Jim Jackson at the hall and you're going to sleep in the cadets' stateroom on board, think of it Kerouac a whole stateroom to yourself, and Mr. Smith has agreed to come with us and celebrate, hm a mahya." —— Mr. Smith was the fat pale potbellied wizard of the bottom skeels of the engine room, a wiper or oiler or general watertender, he was the funniest old guy you'd ever wish to see and already Deni was laughing and feeling good and forgetting the imaginary enemies —— out on the pier street it was evident we were in the clear. Deni was wearing an expensive Hong Kong blue serge suit, with soldiers in his shoulder pads and a fine drape, a beautiful suit, in which, now, beside mine in my road rags, he stomped along like a French farmer throwing his biggest brogans over the rows *de bledeine*, like a Boston hoodlum scuffling along the Common on Saturday night to see the guys at the poolhall but in his own way, with cherubic Deni smile that was heightened tonight by the fog making his face jovial round and red, tho not old, but what with the sun shine of the trip thru the canal he looked like a Dickens character stepping to his post chaise and dusty roads, only what a dismal scene spread before us as we walked.—— Always with Deni it's walking, long long walks, he wouldnt spend a dollar on a cab because he likes to walk but also there were those days when he went out with my first wife and used to shove her right through the subway turnstile before she could realize what happened, from the back naturally —— a charming little trick —— to save a nickel —— a pastime at which old Den's unbeatable, as could be shown —— We came to the Pacific Red Car tracks after a fast hike of about 20 minutes along those dreary refineries and waterskeel slaphouse stop holes, under impossible skies laden I suppose with stars but you could just see their dirty blur in the Southern California Christmas —— "Kerouac we are now at the Pacific Red Car tracks, do you have any faint idea as to what that thing is can you tell that you think you can, but Kerouac you have always struck me as being the funniest man I have ever known . . ."

"No, Deni YOU are the funniest man I ever known ——"

"Dont interrupt, dont drool, dont ——" the way he answered and always talked and he's leading the way across the Red Car tracks, to a hotel, in downtown long Pedro where someone was supposed to meet us with blondes and so he bought enroute a couple of small hand cases of beer for us to portable around with, and when we got to the hotel, which had potted palms and potted barfronts and cars parked, and everything dead and windless with that dead California sad windless smoke-smog, and the Pachucos going by in a hot road and Deni says "You see that bunch of Mexicans in that car with their blue jeans, they got one of our seamen here last Christmas, about a year ago today, he was doing nothing but minding his own business, but they jumped right out that car and beat the living hell out of him —— they take his money —— no money, it's just to be mean, they're Pachucos, they just like to beat up on people for the hell of it ——"

"When I was in Mexico it didnt seem to me the Mexicans there were like that ——"

"The Mexicans in the U.S. is another matter Kerouac, if you'd a been around the world like I have you could see as I do a few of the rough facts of life that apparently with you and the poor people starving in Europe you'll never NEVER under STAAANNND..." gripping my arm again, swinging as he walks, like in our prep school days when we used to go up the sunny morning hill, to Horace Mann, at 246th in Manhattan, on the rock cliffs over by the Van Cortlandt park, the little road, going up thru English halftimber cottages and apartment houses, to the ivied school on top, the whole bunch swinging uphill to school but nobody ever went as fast as Deni as he never paused to take a breath, the climb was very sharp, most had to wind and work and whine and moan along but Deni swung it with his big glad laugh —— In those days he'd sell daggers to the rich little fourth formers, in back of the toilets —— He was up to more tricks tonight —— "Kerouac I'm going to introduce you to two cucamongas in Hollywood tonight if we can get there on time, tomorrow for sure ... two cucamongas living in a house, in an apartment house, the whole thing built clear around a swimmingpool, do you understand what I said, Kerouac? ... a swimmingpool, that you go swimming in ——"

"I know, I know, I seen it in that picture of you and Matthew Peters and all the blondes, great ... What we do, work on em?"

"Wait, a minute, before I explain the rest of the story to you, hand me the gun."

"I havent got the gun you fool, I was only saying that so you'd get off the ship ... I was ready to help you if anything happened."

"YOU HAVENT GOT IT?" It dawned on him he had boasted to the whole crew "My boy's out there on the pier with the gun, what did I tell ya" and he had earler, when the ship left New York, posted a big absurd typically Deni ridiculous poster printed in red ink on a piece of letter paper, "WARNING, THERE ARE FELLOWS ON THE WEST COAST BY THE NAMES OF MATTHEW PETERS AND PAUL LYMAN WOULD LIKE NOTHING BETTER THAN TO CLOBBER THE CARPENTER OF THE ROAMER DENI E. BLEU IF ONLY THEY COULD BUT ANY SHIPMATES OF BLEU WHO WANT TO HELP BE ON THE LOOKOUT FOR THOSE TWO EVIL SCROUNGERS WHEN THE SHIP PUTS IN AT PEDRO AND THERE WILL BE APPRECIATION SIGNED CARPT. FREE DRINKS IN THE CARPT. TONIGHT" —— and then by word in the messroom he'd loudly boasted his boy.

"I knew you'd tell everybody I had the gun, so I said I did. Didnt you feel better walking off the ship?"

"Where is it?"

"I didnt even go."

"Then it's still there. We'll have to pick it up tonight." He was lost in thought —— it was okay.

Deni had big plans for what was going to happen at the hotel, which was the El Carrido Per to Motpaotta Calfiornia potator hotel as I say with potted palmettos and seamen inside and also hotrod champion sons of aircraft computators of Long Beach, the whole general and really dismal California culture a palpable hangout for it, where you saw the dim interiors where you saw the Hawaiian shirted and be-wristwatched, tanned strong young men tilting long thin beers to their mouths and leering and mincing with broads in fancy necklaces and with little white ivory things at their tanned ears and a whole blank blue in their eyes that you saw, also a bestial cruelty hidden and the smell of the beer and smoke and smart smell of the cool inside plush cocktail lounge all that Americanness that in my youth had me get wild to be in it and leave my home and go off be big hero in the American romance-me-jazz night.—— That had made Deni lose his head too, at one time he had been a sad infuriated French boy brought over on a ship to attend American private schools at which time hate smoldered in his bones and in his dark eyes and he wanted to kill the world —— but a little of the Sage and Wisdom education from the Masters of the High West and he wanted to do his hating and killing in cocktail lounges learned from Franchot Tone movies and God knows where and what else.—— We come up to this thing down the drear boulevard, phantasm street with its very bright street lamps and very bright but somber palms jutting out of the sidewalk all pineapple-ribbed and rising into the indefinable California night sky and no wind.—— Inside there was no one to meet Deni as usual mistaken and completely ignored by everyone (good for him but he dont know it) so we have a couple beers, ostensibly waiting, Deni outlines me more facts & personal sophistries, there aint no one coming, no friends, no enemies either, Deni is a perfect Taoist, nothing happens to him, the trouble runs off his shoulders like water, as if he had pig grease on em, he dont know how luck he is, and here he's got his boy at his side old Ti Jean who'll go anywhere follow anyone for adventure.—— Suddenly in the middle of our third or so beer he whoops and realizes we missed the hourly Red Car train and that is going to hold us up another hour in dismal Pedro, we want to get to the glitters of Los Angeles if possible or Hollywood before all the bars closed, in my mind's eye I see all the wonderful things Deni has planned for us there and see, incomprehensible, unrememberable what the images were I was now inventing ere we got going and arrived at the actual scene, not the screen but the dismal four-dimensional scene itself.—— Bang, Deni wants to take a cab and chase the Red Car also with our beer cans in hand

15

cartons we go jogging down the street to a cab stand and hire one to chase the Red Car, which the guy does without comment, knowing the egocentricities of seamen as a O how dismal cabdriver in a O how dismal pierhead jumpin town.—— Off we go —— it's my suspicion he isnt really driving as fast as he ought to actually catch the Red Car, which hiballs right down that line, towards Compton and environs of L.A., at 60 per.—— My suspicion is he doesnt want to get a ticket and at the same time seem to go fast enough to satisfy the whims of the seamen in the back —— it's my suspicion he's just gonna gyp old Den out of a 5 dollar bill.—— Nothing Den likes better than throw away his 5 dollar bills, too —— He thrives on it, he lives for it, he all take voyages around the world working belowdecks among electrical equipment but worse than that take the abuse off officers and men (at four o'clock in the Morning he's asleep in his bunk, "Hey Carptenter, are you the carpenter or are you the chief bottlestopper or shithouse watcher, that goddam forward boom light is out again, I dont know who is using slingshots around here, and but I want that goddam light fixed we'll pulling into Penang in 2 hours and goddam it if it's still dark at that time and I, and we dong got no light it's your ass not mine, see the chief about it") so Deni has to get up, and I can just see him do it, rub the innocent sleep from his eyes and wake to the cold howling world and wish he had a sword so he could cut the man's head off but at the same time he doesnt want to spend the rest of his life in a prison either, or get his own head partially cut off and spend the rest of his life paralyzed with a shoe brace in his neck and people bring him crap pans, so he crawls outa bed and does the bidding of every beast that has every yell to throw at him for every reason in the thousand and one electrical apparati on the goddamn stinking steel jail which as far as I'm

16

concerned, and floating on water too, is what they call a ship.—— What is 5 dollars to a martyr?—— "Step on the gas, we gotta catch that car."

"I'm going fast enough you'll get it." He passes right through Cucamonga. "At exactly 11:38 in 1947 or 1948, one, now I cant remember which one exactly, but I remember I done this for another seaman couple years ago and he passed right through ——" and he goes on talking easing up so's not to pass through the insulting part of just barely beating a red light and I lay back in the seat and say:

"You coulda made that red light, we'll never make it now."

"Listen Jack you wanta make it dontcha and not get fined by some traffic cop."

"Where?" I say looking out the window and all over the horizon at those marshes of night for signs of a cop on a motorcycle or a cruiser —— all you see is marshes and great black distances of night and far off, on hills, the little communities with Christmas lights in their windows blearing red, blearing green, blearing blue, suddenly sending pangs thru me and I think, "Ah America, so big, so sad, so black, you're like the leafs of a dry summer that go crinkly ere August found its end, you're hopeless, everyone you look on you, there's nothing but the dry drear hopelessness, the knowledge of impending death, the suffering of present life, lights of Christmas wont save you or anybody, any more you could put Christmas lights on a dead bush in August, at night, and make it look like something, what is this Christmas you profess, in this void? . . . in this nebulous cloud?"

"That's perfectly alright" says Deni. "Move right along, we'll make it."—— He beats the next light to make it look good but eases up for the next, and up the track and back, you can't see any sign of the rear or the

front of no Red Car, shoot —— he comes to his place
where coupla years ago he'd dropped that seaman, no
Red Car, you can feel its absence, it's come and gone,
empty smell —— You can tell by the electric stillness
on the corner that something just was, & aint.

"Well I guess I missed it, goldang it," says the
cabdriver pushing his hat back to apologize and looking
real hypocritical about it, so Deni gives him five dollars
and we get out and Deni says:

"Kerouac this means we have an hour to wait here
by the cold tracks, in the cold foggy night, for the next
train to L.A."

"That's okay" I say "we got beer aint we, open one
up" and Deni fishes down for the old copper churchkey
and up comes two cans of beer spissing all over the sad
night and we up end the tin, and go slurp —— two cans
each and we start throwing rocks at signs, dancing
around to keep warm, squatting, telling jokes, remembering the past, Deni's going "Hyra rrour Hoo" and
again I hear his great laugh ringing in the American
night and I try to tell him "Deni the reason I followed
the ship all the way 3,200 miles from Staten Island to
goddam Pedro is not only because I wanta get on and
be seen going around the world and have myself a ball
in Port Swettenham and pick up on gangee in Bombay
and find the sleepers and the fluteplayers in filthy Kara-
chi and start revolutions of my own in the Cairo Casbah
and make it from Marseilles to the other side, but because if you, because, the things we used to do, where,
I have a hell of a good time with you Den, there's no
two ways about . . . I never have any money that I admit, I already owe you sixty for the bus fare, but you
must admit I try . . . I'm sorry that I dont have any
money ever, but you know I tried with you, that time . . .
Well goddam, wa ahoo, shit, I want get drunk tonight.——" And Deni says "We dont have to hang

around in the cold like this Jack, look there's a bar, over there" (a roadhouse gleaming redly in the misty night) "it may be a Mexican Pachuco bar and we might get the hell beat out of us but let's go in there and wait the half hour we got with a few beers . . . and see if there're any cucamongas" so we head out to there, across an empty lot. Deni is meanwhile very busy tellin me what a mess I've made of my life but I've heard that from every body coast to coast and I dont care generally and I dont care tonight and this is my way of doing and saying things.

A COUPLA DAYS LATER the S.S. *Roamer* sails away without me because they wouldnt let me get on at the union hall, I had no seniority, all I had to do they said was hang around a couple of months and work on the waterfront or something and wait for a coastwise ship to Seattle and I thought "So if I'm gonna travel coasts I'm going to go down the coast I covet."—— So I see the Roamer slipping out of Pedro bay, at night again, the red port light and the green starboard light sneaking across the water with attendant ghostly following mast lights, vup! (the whistle of the little tug) —— then the ever Gandharva-like, illusion-and-Maya-like dimlights of the portholes where some members of the crew are reading in bunks, others eating snacks in the crew mess, and others, like Deni, eagerly writing letters with a big red ink fountain pen assuring me that next time around the world I will get on the Roamer.—— "But I dont care, I'll go to Mexico" says I and walk off to the Pacific Red Car waving at Deni's ship vanishing out there . . .

Among the madcap pranks we'd pulled after that first night I told you about, we carried a huge tumble-weed up the gangplank at 3 A M Christmas Eve and shoved it into the engine crew foc'sle (where they were all snoring) and left it there.—— When they woke up in the morning they thought they were somewhere else, in the jungle or something, and all went back to bed.—— So when the Chief Engineer is yelling "Who the hell put that tree on board!" (it was ten feet by ten feet, a big ball of dry twigs), way off across and down the ship's iron heart you hear Deni howling "Hoo hoo hoo! *Who the hell put that tree on board! Oh that Chief Engineer is a very funny* m-a-h-n!"

2. MEXICO FELLAHEEN

WHEN YOU GO ACROSS THE BORDER at Nogales Arizona some very severe looking American
guards, some of them pasty faced with sinister steelrim
spectacles go scrounging through all your beat baggage
for signs of the scorpion of scofflaw.—— You just wait
patiently like you always do in America among those
apparently endless policemen and their endless laws
against (no laws *for*) —— but the moment you cross the
little wire gate and you're in Mexico, you feel like you
just sneaked out of school when you told the teacher
you were sick and she told you you could go home, 2
o'clock in the afternoon.—— You feel as though you just
come home from Sunday morning church and you take
off your suit and slip into your soft worn smooth cool
overalls, to play —— you look around and you see happy
smiling faces, or the absorbed dark faces of worried
lovers and fathers and policemen, you hear cantina music
from across the little park of balloons and popsicles.——

In the middle of the little park is a bandstand for concerts, actual concerts for the people, free —— generations
of marimba players maybe, or an Orozco jazzband playing Mexican anthems to El Presidente.—— You walk
thirsty through the swinging doors of a saloon and get
a bar beer, and turn around and there's fellas shooting
pool, cooking tacos, wearing sombreros, some wearing
guns on their rancher hips, and gangs of singing businessmen throwing pesos at the standing musicians who wander up and down the room.—— It's a great feeling of
entering the Pure Land, especially because it's so close
to dry faced Arizona and Texas and all over the South-
west —— but you can find it, this feeling, this fellaheen
feeling about life, that timeless gayety of people not involved in great cultural and civilization issues —— you
can find it almost anywhere else, in Morocco, in Latin
America entire, in Dakar, in Kurd land.——

There is no "violence" in Mexico, that was all a
lot of bull written up by Hollywood writers or writers
who went to Mexico to "be violent" —— I know of an
American who went to Mexico for bar brawls because
you dont usually get arrested there for disorderly con-
duct, my God I've seen men wrestle playfully in the
middle of the road blocking traffic, screaming with
laughter, as people walked by smiling —— Mexico is
generally gentle and fine, even when you travel among
the dangerous characters as I did —— "dangerous" in
the sense we mean in America —— in fact the further
you go away from the border, and deeper down, the
finer it is, as though the influence of civilizations hung
over the border like a cloud.

THE EARTH IS AN INDIAN THING —— I
squatted on it, rolled thick sticks of marijuana on sod
floors of stick huts not far from Mazatlan near the

opium center of the world and we sprinkled opium in our masterjoints —— we had black heels. We talked about Revolution. The host was of the opinion the Indians originally owned North America just as well as South America, about time to come out and say *"La tierra esta la notre"* —— (the earth is ours) —— which he did, clacking his tongue and with a hip sneer hunching up his mad shoulders for us to see his doubt and mistrust of anyone understanding what he meant but I was there and understood quite well.—— In the corner an Indian woman, 18, sat, partly behind the table, her face in the shadows of the candle glow —— she was watching us high either on "O" or herself as wife of a man who in the morning went out in the yard with a spear and split sticks on the ground idly languidly throwing it ground down half-turning to gesture and say something to his partner.—— The drowsy hum of Fellaheen Village at noon —— not far away was the sea, warm, the tropical Pacific of Cancer.—— Spine-ribbed mountains all the way from Calexico and Shasta and Modoc and Columbia River Pasco-viewing sat rumped behind the plain upon which this coast was laid.—— A one thousand mile dirt road led there —— quiet buses 1931 thin high style goofy with oldfashioned clutch handles leading to floor holes, old side benches for seats, turned around, solid wood, bouncing in interminable dust down past the Navajoas, Margaritas and general pig desert dry huts of Doctor Pepper and pig's eye on tortilla half burned —— tortured road —— led to this the capital of the world kingdom of opium —— Ah Jesus —— I looked at my host.—— On the sod floor, in a corner, snored a soldier of the Mexican Army, it was a revolution. The Indian was mad. *"La Tierra esta la notre ——"*

Enrique my guide and buddy who couldnt say "H" but had to say "K" —— because his nativity was not buried in the Spanish name of Vera Cruz his hometown,

in the Mixtecan Tongue instead.—— On buses joggling
in eternity he kept yelling at me "HK-o-t? HK-o-t? Is
means *caliente*. Unnerstan?"

"Yeah yeah."

"Is k-o-t . . . is k-o-t . . . is means *caliente* —— HK-
eat. . . . eat . . ."

"H-eat!"

"Is what letter —— alphabay?"

"H"

"Is . . . HK . . . ?"

"No . . . H . . ."

"Is Kard for me to pronouse. I can' do it."

When he said "K" his whole jaw leaped out, I saw
the Indian in his face. He now squatted in the sod explaining eagerly to the host who by his tremendous de-
meanor I knew to be the King of some regal gang laid
out in the desert, by his complete sneering speech concerning every subject brought up, as if by blood king
by right, trying to persuade, or protect, or ask for something, I sat, said nothing, watched, like Gerardo in the
corner.—— Gerardo was listening with astonished air
at his big brother make a mad speech in front of the
King and under the circumstances of the strange Ameri-
cano Gringo with his seabag. He nodded and leered like
an old merchant the host to hear it and turned to his
wife and showed his tongue and licked his lower teeth
and then damped top teeth on lip, to make a quick sneer
into the unknown Mexican dark overhead the candlelight hut under Pacific Coast Tropic of Cancer stars like
in Acapulco fighting name.—— The moon washed rocks
from El Capitan on down —— The swamps of Panama
later on and soon enough.

Pointing, with huge arm, finger, the host: —— "Is
in the rib of mountains of the big plateau! the golds of
war are buried deep! the caves bleed! we'll take the
snake out of the woods! we'll tear the wings off the great

bird! we shall live in the iron houses overturned in fields of rags!"

"*Si!*" said our quiet friend from the edge of the pallet cot. Estrando.—— Goatee, hip eyes drooping brown sad and narcotic, opium, hands falling, strange witchdoctor sitter-next-to of this King —— threw in occasional remarks that had the others listening but whenever he tried to follow through it was no go, he overdid something, he dulled them, they refused to listen to his elaborations and artistic touches in the brew.—— Primeval carnal sacrifice is what they wanted. No anthropologist should forget the cannibals, or avoid the Auca. Get me a bow and arrow and I'll go; I'm ready now; plane fare please; plain fare; vacuous is the list; knights grow bold growing old; young knights dream.

Soft.—— Our Indian King wanted nothing to do with tentative ideas; he listened to Enrique's real pleas, took note of Estrando's hallucinated sayings, guttural remarks spicy thrown in pithy like madness inward and from which the King had learned all he knew of what reality would think of him —— he eyed me with honest suspicion.

In Spanish I heard him ask if this Gringo was some cop following him from L.A., some F.B.I. man. I heard and said no. Enrique tried to tell him I was *interessa* pointing at his own head to mean I was interested in things —— I was trying to learn Spanish, I was a head, *cabeza,* also *chucharro* —— (potsmoker).—— *Chucharro* didnt interest King. In L.A. he'd gone walking in from the Mexican darkness on bare feet palms out black face to the lights —— somebody's ripped a crucifix chain from his neck, some cop or hoodlum, he snarled remembering it, his revenge was either silent or someone was left dead and I was the F.B.I. man —— the weird follower of Mexican suspects with records of having left feet prints on the sidewalks of Iron L.A. and chains in jail-

25

houses and potential revolutionary heroes of late afternoon mustaches in the reddy soft light.——

He showed me a pellet of O.—— I named it.—— Partially satisfied. Enrique pleaded further in my defense. The witchdoctor smiled inwardly, he had no time to goof or do court dances or sing of drink in whore alleys looking for pimps —— he was Goethe in the court of Fredericko Weimar.—— Vibrations of television telepathy surrounded the room as silently the King decided to accept me —— when he did I heard the sceptre drop in all their thoughts.

And O the holy sea of Mazatlan and the great red plain of eve with burros and aznos and red and brown horses and green cactus pulque.

The three *muchachas* two miles away in a little group talking in the exact concentric center of the circle of the red universe —— the softness of their speech could never reach us, nor these waves of Mazatlan destroy it by their bark —— soft sea winds to beautify the weed —— three islands one mile out —— rocks —— the Fellaheen City's muddy rooftops dusk in back . . .

TO EXPLAIN, I'D MISSED THE SHIP in San Pedro and this was the midway point of the trip from the Mexican border at Nogales Arizona that I had undertaken on cheap second class buses all the way down the West Coast to Mexico City.—— I'd met Enrique and his kid brother Gerardo while the passengers were stretching their legs at desert huts in the Sonora desert where big fat Indian ladies served hot tortillas and meat off stone stoves and as you stood there waiting for your sandwich the little pigs grazed lovingly against your legs.—— Enrique was a great sweet kid with black hair and black eyes who was making this epic journey all the way to Vera Cruz two thousand miles away on the Gulf of Mexico with his kid brother for some reason I never found out —— all he let me know was that inside his home made wooden radio set was hidden about a half a pound of strong dark green marijuana with the moss still in it and long black hairs in it, the sign of good pot.—— We immediately started blasting among the cacti in the back of the desert waystations, squatting there in the hot sun laughing, as Gerardo watched (he was only 18 and wasnt allowed to smoke by his older brother) —— "Is why? because marijuana is bad for the eye and bad for *la ley*" (bad for the eyesight and bad for the law) —— "But jew!" pointing at me (Mexican saying "you"), "and *me!*" pointing at himself, "we alright." He undertook to be my guide in the great trip through the continental spaces of Mexico —— he spoke some English and tried to explain to me the epic grandeur of his land and I certainly agreed with him.—— "See?" he'd say pointing at distant mountain ranges. "*Mehico!*"

The bus was an old high thin affair with wooden benches, as I say, and passengers in shawls and straw hats got on with their goats or pigs or chickens while kids rode on the roof or hung on singing and screaming from the tailgate.—— We bounced and bounced over that one thousand mile dirt road and when we came to rivers the driver just plowed through the shallow water, washing off the dust, and bounced on.—— Strange towns like Navajoa where I took a walk by myself and saw, in the market outdoor affair, a butcher standing in front of a pile of lousy beef for sale, flies swarming all over it while mangy skinny fellaheen dogs scrounged around under the table —— and towns like Los Mochis (The Flies) where we sat drinking Orange Crush like grandees at sticky little tables, where the day's headline in the Los Mochis newspaper told of a midnight gun duel between the Chief of Police and the Mayor —— it was all

over town, some excitement in the white alleys ——
both of them with revolvers on their hips, bang, blam,
right in the muddy street outside the cantina.—— Now
we were in a town further south in Sinaloa and had gotten off the old bus at midnight to walk single file through
the slums and past the bars ("Ees no good you and me
and Gerardo go into cantina, ees bad for *la ley*" said
Enrique) and then, Gerardo carrying my seabag on his
back like a true friend and brother, we crossed a great
empty plaza of dirt and came to a bunch of stick huts
forming a little village not far from the soft starlit
surf, and there we knocked on the door of that mustachio'd wild man with the opium and were admitted to
his candlelit kitchen where he and his witchdoctor
goatee Estrando were sprinkling red pinches of pure
opium into huge cigarettes of marijuana the size of a
cigar.

The host allowed us to sleep the night in the little
grass hut nearby —— this hermitage belonged to Estrando, who was very kind to let us sleep there —— he
showed us in by candlelight, removed his only belongings which consisted of his opium stash under the pallet on the sod where he slept, and crept off to sleep
somewhere else.—— We had only one blanket and
tossed to see who would have to sleep in the middle: it
was the kid Gerardo, who didnt complain.—— In the
morning I got up and peeked out through the sticks: it
was a drowsy sweet little grass hut village with lovely
brown maids carrying jugs of water from the main
well on their shoulders —— smoke of tortillas rose
among the trees —— dogs barked, children played, and
as I say our host was up and splitting twigs with a spear
by throwing the spear to the ground neatly parting the
twigs (or thin boughs) clean in half, an amazing sight.
—— And when I wanted to go to the john I was di-
rected to an ancient stone seat which overlorded the

28

entire village like some king's throne and there I had to
sit in full sight of everybody, it was completely in the
open —— mothers passing by smiled politely, children
stared with fingers in mouth, young girls hummed at
their work.

We began packing to get back on the bus and carry
on to Mexico City but first I bought a quarter pound of
marijuana but as soon as the deal was done in the hut
a file of Mexican soldiers and a few seedy policemen
came in with sad eyes.—— I said to Enrique: "Hey, are
we going to be arrested?" He said no, they just wanted
some of the marijuana for themselves, free, and would
let us go peaceably.—— So Enrique cut them into about
half of what we had and they squatted all around the
hut and rolled joints on the ground.—— I was so sick on
an opium hangover I lay there staring at everybody
feeling like I was about to be skewered, have my arms
cut off, hung upsidedown on the cross and burned at
the stake on that high stone john.—— Boys brought me
soup with hot peppers in it and everybody smiled as I
sipped it, lying on my side —— it burned into my throat,
made me gasp, cough and sneeze, and instantly I felt
better.

We got up and Gerardo again heaved my seabag
to his back, Enrique hid the marijuana in his wooden
radio, we shook hands with our host and the witchdoctor
solemnly, shook hands seriously and solemnly with
every one of the ten policemen and cop soldiers and
off we went single file again in the hot sun towards the
bus station in town.—— "Now," said Enrique patting
the home made radio, "see, *mir*, we all set to get high."

The sun was very hot and we were sweating ——
we came to a large beautiful church in the old Spanish
Mission style and Enrique said: "We go in here now"
—— it amazed me to remember that we were all Catho-
lics.—— We went inside and Gerardo kneeled first, then

Enrique and I kneed the pews and did the sign of the cross and he whispered in my ear "See? is cool in the chorch. Is good to get away from the sun a *minuto*."

At Mazatlan at dusk we stopped for awhile for a swim in our underwear in that magnificent surf and it was there, on the beach, with a big joint smoking in his hand where Enrique turned and pointed inland at the beautiful green fields of Mexico and said "See the three girls in the middle of the field far away?" and I looked and looked and only barely saw three dots in the middle of a distant pasture. "Three muchachas," said Enrique. "Is mean: *Mehico!*"

He wanted me to go to Vera Cruz with him. "I am a shoemaker by trade. You stay home with the gurls while I work, *mir?* You write you *interessa* books and we get lots of gurls."

I never saw him after Mexico City because I had no money absolutely and I had to stay on William Seward Burroughs' couch. And Burroughs didnt want Enrique around: "You shouldnt hang around with these Mexicans, they're all a bunch of con men."

I still have the rabbit's foot Enrique gave me when he left.

A FEW WEEKS LATER I go to see my first bull-fight, which I must confess is a *novillera*, a novice fight, and not the real thing they show in the winter which is supposed to be so artistic. Inside it is a perfect round bowl with a neat circle of brown dirt being harrowed and raked by expert loving rakers like the man who rakes second base in Yankee Stadium only this is Bite-the-Dust Stadium.—— When I sat down the bull had just come in and the orchestra was sitting down again. —— Fine embroidered clothes tightly fitted to boys behind a fence.—— Solemn they were, as a big beautiful

shiny black bull rushed out gallumphing from a corner
I hadnt looked, where he'd been apparently mooing for
help, black nostrils and big white eyes and outspread
horns, all chest no belly, stove polish thin legs seeking
to drive the earth down with all that locomotive weight
above —— some people sniggered —— bull galloped and
flashed, you saw the riddled-up muscle holes in his perfect prize skin.—— Matador stepped out and invited and
the bull charged and slammed in, matador sneered his
cape, let pass the horns by his loins a foot or two, got
the bull revolved around by cape, and walked away like
a Grandee —— and stood his back to the dumb perfect
bull who didnt charge like in "Blood & Sand" and lift
Señor Grandee into the upper deck. Then business got
underway. Out comes the old pirate horse with patch on
eye, picador KNIGHT aboard with a lance, to come and
dart a few slivers of steel in the bull's shoulderblade
who responds by trying to lift the horse but the horse
is mailed (thank God) —— a historical and crazy scene
except suddenly you realize the picador has started the
bull on his interminable bleeding. The blinding of the
poor bull in mindless vertigo is continued by the brave
bowlegged little dart man carrying two darts with rib-
bon, here he comes head-on at the bull, the bull head-on
for him, wham, no head-on crash for the dart man has
stung with dart and darted away before you can say boo
(& I did say boo), because a bull is hard to dodge? Good
enough, but the darts now have the bull streaming with
blood like Marlowe's Christ in the heavens.—— An old
matador comes out and tests the bull with a few capes'
turn then another set of darts, a battleflag now shining
down the living breathing suffering bull's side and everybody *glad*.—— And now the bull's charge is just a stagger and so now the serious hero matador comes out for
the kill as the orchestra goes one boom-lick on bass drum,
it get quiet like a cloud passing over the sun, you hear

a drunkard's bottle smash a mile away in the cruel Spanish green aromatic countryside —— children pause over tortas —— the bull stands in the sun head-bowed, panting for life, his sides actually *flapping* against his ribs, his shoulders barbed like San Sebastian.—— The careful footed matador youth, brave enough in his own right, approaches and curses and the bull rolls around and comes stoggling on wobbly feet at the red cape, dives in with blood streaming everywhichaway and the boy just accommodates him through the imaginary hoop and circles and hangs on tiptoe, knockkneed. And Lord, I didnt want to see his smooth tight belly ranted by no horn.—— He rippled his cape again at the bull who just stood there thinking "O why cant I go home?" and the matador moved closer and now the animal bunched tired legs to run but one leg slipped throwing up a cloud of dust.—— But he dove in and flounced off to rest.—— The matador draped his sword and called the humble bull with glazed eyes.—— The bull pricked his ears and didnt move.—— The matador's whole body stiffened like a board that shakes under the trample of many feet —— a muscle showed in his stocking.—— Bull plunged a feeble three feet and turned in dust and the matador arched his back in front of him like a man leaning over a hot stove to reach for something on the other side and flipped his sword a yard deep into the bull's shoulderblade separation.—— Matador walked one way, bull the other with sword to hilt and staggered, started to run, looked up with human surprise at the sky & sun, and then gargled —— O go see it folks!—— He threw up ten gallons of blood into the air and it splashed all over —— he fell on his knees choking on his own blood and spewed and twisted his neck around and suddenly got floppy doll and his head blammed flat.—— He still wasnt dead, an extra idiot rushed out and knifed him with a wren-like dagger in the neck nerve and still the bull dug the sides of his poor mouth in the sand and chewed old blood.—— His eyes! O his eyes!—— Idiots sniggered because the dagger did this, as though it would not.—— A team of hysterical horses were rushed out to chain and drag the bull away, they galloped off but the chain broke and the bull slid in dust like a dead fly kicked unconsciously by a foot.—— Off, off with him! —— He's gone, white eyes staring the last thing you see.—— Next bull!—— First the old boys shovel blood in a wheel-barrow and rush off with it. The quiet raker returns with his rake —— "Ole!," girls throwing flowers at the animal-murder in the fine britches.—— And I saw how everybody dies and nobody's going to care, I felt how awful it is to live just so you can die like a bull trapped in a screaming human ring.——

Jai Alai, Mexico, Jai Alai!

THE LAST DAY I'M IN MEXICO I'm in the little church near Redondas in Mexico City, 4 o'clock in the gray afternoon, I've walked all over town delivering packages at the Post Offices and I've munched on fudge candy for breakfast and now, with two beers under me, I'm resting in the church contemplating the void.

Right above me is a great tormented statue of Christ on the Cross, when I first saw it I instantly sat under it, after brief standing hand-clasped look at it —— ("Jeanne!" they call me in the courtyard and it's for some other Lady, I run to the door and look out).—— "Mon Jésus," I'm saying, and I look up and there He is, they've put on Him a handsome face like young Robert Mitchum and have closed His eyes in death tho one of them is slightly open you think and it also looks like young Robert Mitchum or Enrique high on tea looking at you thru the smoke and saying "Hombre, man, this is the end."—— His knees are all scratched so hard sore they're scathed wore out through, an inch deep the hole where His kneecap's been wailed away by flailing falls on them with the big Flail Cross a hundred miles long on His back, and as He leans there with the Cross on rocks they goad Him on to slide on His knees and He's worn them out by the time He's nailed to the cross —— I was there.—— Shows the big rip in His ribs where the sword-tips of lancers were stuck up at Him.—— I was not there, had I been there I would have yelled "Stop it" and got crucified too.—— Here Holy Spain has sent the bloodheart sacrifice Aztecs of Mexico a picture of tenderness and pity, saying, "This you would do to Man? I am the Son of Man, I am of Man, I am Man and this you would do to Me, Who Am Man and God —— I am God, and you would pierce my feet bound together with long nails with big stayfast points on the end slightly blunted by the hammerer's might —— this you did to Me, and I preached Love?"

He Preached love, and you would have him bound to a tree and hammered into it with nails, you fools, you should be forgiven.

It shows the blood running from His hands to His armpits and down His sides.—— The Mexicans have hung a graceful canopy of red velvet around His loins, it's too high a statue for there to have been pinners of medals on That Holy Victory Cloth ——

What a Victory, the Victory of Christ! Victory over madness, mankind's blight. "Kill him!" they still roar at fights, cockfights, bullfights, prizefights, streetfights, fieldfights, airfights, wordfights —— "Kill him!" —— Kill the Fox, the Pig and the Pox.

Christ in His Agony, pray for me.

It shows His body falling from the Cross on His hand of nails, the perfect slump built in by the artist, the devout sculptor who worked on this with all his heart, the Compassion and tenacity of a Christ —— a sweet perhaps Indian Spanish Catholic of the 15th century, among ruins of adobe and mud and stinksmokes of Indian mid millenium in North America, devised this *statuo del Cristo* and pinned it up in the new church which now, 1950's, four hundred years later or five, has lost portions of the ceiling where some Spanish Michelangelo has run up cherubs and angelkins for the edification of upward gazers on Sunday mornings when the kind Padre expostulates on the details of the law religious.

I pray on my knees so long, looking up sideways at my Christ, I suddenly wake up in a trance in the church with my knees aching and a sudden realization that I've been listening to a profound buzz in my ears that permeates throughout the church and throughout my ears and head and throughout the universe, the intrinsic silence of Purity (which is Divine). I sit in the pew quietly, rubbing my knees, the silence is roaring.——

Ahead is the Altar, the Virgin Mary is white in a field of blue-and-white-and-golden arrangements —— it's too far to see adequately, I promise myself to go forward to the altar as soon as some of the people leave. —— The people are all women, young and old, and suddenly here come two children in rags and blankets and barefooted walking slowly down the right hand aisle with the big boy laying his hand anxiously holding something on his little brother's head, I wonder why —— they're both barefooted but I hear the clack of heels, I wonder why —— they go forward to the altar, come around the side to the glass coffin of a saint statue, all the time walking slowly, anxiously, touching everything, looking up, crawling infinitesimally around the church and taking it all in completely.—— At the coffin the littler boy (3 years old) touches the glass and goes around to the foot of the dead and touches the glass and I think "They understand death, they stand there in

35

the church under the skies that have a beginningless past and go into the never-ending future, waiting themselves for death, at the foot of the dead, in a holy temple." —— I get a vision of myself and the two little boys hung up in a great endless universe with nothing overhead and nothing under but the Infinite Nothingness, the Enormousness of it, the dead without number in all directions of existence whether inward into the atomworlds of your own body or outward to the universe which may only be one atom in an infinity of atomworlds and each atom world only a figure of speech —— inward, outward, up and down, nothing but emptiness and divine majesty and silence for the two little boys and me.—— Anxiously I watch them leave, to my amaze I see a little tiny girl one foot or and-a-half high, two years old, or one-and-a-half, waddling tinily lowly beneath them, a meek little lamb on the floor of the church. Anxiousness of big brother was to hold a shawl over her head, he wanted little brother to hold *his* end, between them and under the canopy marched Princessa Sweetheart examining the church with her big brown eyes, her little heels clacking.

As soon as they're outside, they play with the other children. Many children are playing in the garden-enclosed entryway, some of them are standing and staring at the upper front of the church at images of angels in rain dimmed stone.

I bow to all this, kneel at my pew entryway, and go out, taking one last look at St. Antoine de Padue (St. Anthony) Santo Antonio de Padua.—— Everything is perfect on the street again, the world is permeated with roses of happiness all the time, but none of us know it. The happiness consists in realizing that it is all a great strange dream.

3. THE RAILROAD EARTH

THERE WAS A LITTLE ALLEY in San Francisco back of the Southern Pacific station at Third and Townsend in redbrick of drowsy lazy afternoons with everybody at work in offices in the air you feel the impending rush of their commuter frenzy as soon they'll be charging en masse from Market and Sansome buildings on foot and in buses and all well-dressed thru workingman Frisco of Walkup ?? truck drivers and even the poor grime-bemarked Third Steet of lost bums even Negroes so hopeless and long left East and meanings of responsibility and *try* that now all they do is stand there spitting in the broken glass sometimes fifty in one afternoon against one wall at Third and Howard and here's all these Millbrae and San Carlos neat-necktied producers and commuters of America and Steel civilization rushing by with San Francisco *Chronicles* and green *Call-Bulletins* not even enough time to be disdainful, they've got to catch 130, 132, 134, 136 all the way up to 146 till the time of evening supper in homes of the railroad earth when high in the sky the magic stars ride above the following hotshot freight trains.—— It's all in California, it's all a sea, I swim out of it in afternoons of sun hot meditation in my jeans with head on handkerchief on brakeman's lantern or (if not working) on books, I look up at blue sky of perfect lostpurity and feel the warp of wood of old America beneath me and have insane conversations with Negroes in several-story windows above and everything is pouring in, the switching moves of boxcars in that little alley which is so much like the alleys of Lowell and I hear far off in the sense of coming night that engine calling our mountains.

BUT IT WAS THAT BEAUTIFUL CUT of clouds I could always see above the little S.P. alley, puffs floating by from Oakland or the Gate of Marin to the north or San Jose south, the clarity of Cal to break your heart. It was the fantastic drowse and drum hum of lum mum afternoon nathin' to do, ole Frisco with end of land sadness —— the people —— the alley full of trucks and cars of businesses nearabouts and nobody knew or far from cared who I was all my life three thousand five hundred miles from birth-O opened up and at last belonged to me in Great America.

Now it's night in Third Street the keen little neons and also yellow bulblights of impossible-to-believe flops with dark ruined shadows moving back of torn yellow shades like a degenerate China with no money —— the cats in Annie's Alley, the flop comes on, moans, rolls, the street is loaded with darkness. Blue sky above with stars hanging high over old hotel roofs and blowers of hotels moaning out dusts of interior, the grime inside the word in mouths falling out tooth by tooth, the reading rooms tick tock bigclock with creak chair and slant-

boards and old faces looking up over rimless spectacles
bought in some West Virginia or Florida or Liverpool
England pawnshop long before I was born and across
rains they've come to the end of the land sadness end
of the world gladness all you San Franciscos will have
to fall eventually and burn again. But I'm walking and
one night a bum fell into the hole of the construction
job where theyre tearing a sewer by day the husky
Pacific & Electric youths in torn jeans who work there
often I think of going up to some of em like say blond
ones with wild hair and torn shirts and say "You oughta
apply for the railroad its much easier work you dont
stand around the street all day and you get much more
pay" but this bum fell in the hole you saw his foot stick
out, a British MG also driven by some eccentric once
backed into the hole and as I came home from a long
Saturday afternoon local to Hollister out of San Jose
miles away across verdurous fields of prune and juice
joy here's this British MG backed and legs up wheels
up into a pit and bums and cops standing around right
outside the coffee shop —— it was the way they fenced
it but he never had the nerve to do it due to the fact
that he had no money and nowhere to go and O his
father was dead and O his mother was dead and O his
sister was dead and O his whereabout was dead was
dead.—— But and then at that time also I lay in my
room on long Saturday afternoons listening to Jumpin'
George with my fifth of tokay no tea and just under the
sheets laughed to hear the crazy music "Mama, he treats
your daughter mean," Mama, Papa, and dont you come
in here I'll kill you etc. getting high by myself in room
glooms and all wondrous knowing about the Negro the
essential American out there always finding his solace
his meaning in the fellaheen street and not in abstract
morality and even when he has a church you see the
pastor out front bowing to the ladies on the make you

hear his great vibrant voice on the sunny Sunday afternoon sidewalk full of sexual vibratos saying "Why yes
Mam but de gospel do say that man was born of woman's
womb ——" and no and so by that time I come crawling
out of my warmsack and hit the street when I see the
railroad ain't gonna call me till 5 AM Sunday morn
probably for a local out of Bayshore in fact always for
a local out of Bayshore and I go to the wailbar of all
the wildbars in the world the one and only Third-and-
Howard and there I go in and drink with the madmen
and if I get drunk I git.

The whore who come up to me in there the night
I was there with Al Buckle and said to me "You wanta
play with me tonight Jim, and?" and I didnt think I
had enough money and later told this to Charley Low
and he laughed and said "How do you know she wanted
money always take the chance that she might be out just
for love or just out for love you know what I mean
man dont be a sucker." She was a goodlooking doll and
said "How would you like to oolyakoo with me mon?"
and I stood there like a jerk and in fact bought drink
got drink drunk that night and in the 299 Club I was
hit by the proprietor the band breaking up the fight before I had a chance to decide to hit him back which I
didnt do and out on the street I tried to rush back in
but they had locked the door and were looking at me
thru the forbidden glass in the door with faces like
undersea —— I should have played with her shurro-
uruuruuruuruuruuruuruurkdiei.

DESPITE THE FACT I WAS A BRAKEMAN
making 600 a month I kept going to the Public restaurant on Howard Street which was three eggs for 26
cents 2 eggs for 21 this with toast (hardly no butter)
coffee (hardly no coffee and sugar rationed) oatmeal

with dash of milk and sugar the smell of soured old shirts lingering above the cookpot steams as if they were making skidrow lumberjack stews out of San Francisco ancient Chinese mildewed laundries with poker games in the back among the barrels and the rats of the earthquake days, but actually the food somewhat on the level of an oldtime 1890 or 1910 section-gang cook of lumber camps far in the North with an oldtime pigtail Chinaman cooking it and cussing out those who didnt like it. The prices were incredible but one time I had the beefstew and it was absolutely the worst beefstew I ever et, it was incredible I tell you —— and as they often did that to me it was with the most intensest regret that I tried to convey to the geek back of counter what I wanted but he was a tough sonofabitch, ech, ti-ti, I thought the counterman was kind of queer especially he handled gruffly the hopeless drooldrunks, "What now you doing you think you can come in here and cut like that for God's sake act like a man won't you and eat or get out-t-t-t-" —— I always did wonder what a guy like that was doing working in a place like that because, but why some sympathy in his horny heart for the busted wrecks, all up and down the street were restaurants like the Public catering exclusively to bums of the black, winos with no money, who found 21 cents left over from wine panhandlings and so stumbled in for their third or fourth touch of food in a week, as sometimes they didnt eat at all and so you'd see them in the corner puking white liquid which was a couple quarts of rancid sauterne rotgut or sweet white sherry and they had nothing on their stomachs, most of them had one leg or were on crutches and had bandages around their feet, from nicotine and alcohol poisoning together, and one time finally on my way up Third near Market across the street from Breens, when in early 1952 I lived on Russian Hill and didnt quite dig the complete horror

and humor of railroad's Third Street, a bum a thin
sickly littlebum like Anton Abraham lay face down on
the pavement with crutch aside and some old remnant
newspaper sticking out and it seemed to me he was dead.
I looked closely to see if he was breathing and he was
not, another man with me was looking down and we
agreed he was dead, and soon a cop came over and took
and agreed and called the wagon, the little wretch
weighed about 50 pounds in his bleeding count and was
stone mackerel snotnose cold dead as a bleeding door-
nail —— ah I tell you —— and who could notice but
other half dead deadbums bums bums bums dead dead
times X times X times all dead bums forever dead with
nothing and all finished and out —— there.—— And this
was the clientele in the Public Hair restaurant where I
ate many's the morn a 3-egg breakfast with almost dry
toast and oatmeal a little saucer of, and thin sickly dish-
water coffee, all to save 14 cents so in my little book
proudly I could make a notation and of the day and
prove that I could live comfortably in America while
working seven days a week and earning 600 a month
I could live on less that 17 a week which with my rent
of 4.20 was okay as I had also to spend money to eat
and sleep sometimes on the other end of my Watsonville chaingang run but preferred most times to sleep
free of charge and uncomfortable in cabooses of the
crummy rack —— my 26-cent breakfast, my pride.——
And that incredible semiqueer counterman who dished
out the food, threw it at you, slammed it, had a languid
frank expression straight in your eyes like a 1930's lunch-
cart heroine in Steinbeck and at the steamtable itself
labored coolly a junkey-looking Chinese with an actual
stocking in his hair as if they'd just Shanghai'd him off
the foot of Commercial Street before the Ferry Building was up but forgot it was 1952, dreamed it was 1860

42

goldrush Frisco —— and on rainy days you felt they had ships in the back room.

I'D TAKE WALKS UP HARRISON and the boom-crash of truck traffic towards the glorious girders of the Oakland Bay Bridge that you could see after climbing Harrison Hill a little like radar machine of eternity in the sky, huge, in the blue, by pure clouds crossed, gulls, idiot cars streaking to destinations on its undinal boom across shmoshwaters flocked up by winds and news of San Rafael storms and flash boats.—— There O I always came and walked and negotiated whole Friscos in one afternoon from the overlooking hills of the high Fillmore where Orient-bound vessels you can see on drowsy Sunday mornings of poolhall goof like after a whole night playing drums in a jam session and a morn in the hall of cuesticks I went by the rich homes of old ladies supported by daughters or female secretaries with immense ugly gargoyle Frisco millions fronts of other days and way below is the blue passage of the Gate, the Alcatraz mad rock, the mouths of Tamalpais, San Pablo Bay, Sausalito sleepy hemming the rock and bush over yonder, and the sweet white ships cleanly cutting a path to Sasebo.—— Over Harrison and down to the Embarcadero and around Telegraph Hill and up the back of Russian Hill and down to the play streets of Chinatown and down Kearney back across Market to Third and my wild-night neon twinkle fate there, ah, and then finally at dawn of a Sunday and they did call me, the immense girders of Oakland Bay still haunting me and all that eternity too much to swallow and not knowing who I am at all but like a big plump longhaired baby walking up in the dark trying to wonder who I am the door knocks and it's the desk keeper of the flop hotel with silver rims and white hair and clean clothes and sickly potbelly said he was from Rocky Mount and looked like yes, he had been desk clerk of the Nash Buncome Association hotel down there in 50 successive heatwave summers without the sun and only palmos of the lobby with cigar crutches in the albums of the South and him with his dear mother waiting in a buried log cabin of graves with all that mashed past historied underground afoot with the stain of the bear the blood of the tree and cornfields long plowed under and Negroes whose voices long faded from the middle of the wood and the dog barked his last, this man had voyageured to the West Coast too like all the other loose American elements and was pale and sixty and complaining of sickness, might at one time been a handsome squire to women with money but now a forgotten clerk and maybe spent a little time in jail for a few forgeries or harmless cons and might also have been a railroad clerk and might have wept and might have never made it, and that day I'd say he saw the bridgegirders up over the hill of traffic of Harrison like me and woke up mornings with same lost, is now beckoning on my door and breaking in the world on me and he is standing on the frayed carpet of the hall all worn down by black steps of sunken old men for last 40 years since earthquake and the toilet stained, beyond the last toilet bowl and the last stink and stain I guess yes is the end of the world the bloody end of the world, so now knocks on my door and I wake up, saying "How what howp howelk howel of the knavery they've meaking, ek and wont let me slepit? Whey they dool? Whand out wisis thing that comes flarminging around my dooring in the mouth of the night and there everything knows that I have no mother, and no sister, and no father and no bot sosstle, but not crib" I get up and sit up and says "Howowow?" and he says "Telephone?" and I have to put on my

jeans heavy with knife, wallet, I look closely at my railroad watch hanging on little door flicker of closet door
face to me ticking silent the time, it says 4:30 AM of
a Sunday morn, I go down the carpet of the skidrow
hall in jeans and with no shirt and yes with shirt tails
hanging gray workshirt and pick up phone and ticky
sleepy night desk with cage and spittoons and keys hanging and old towels piled clean ones but frayed at edges
and bearing names of every hotel of the moving prime,
on the phone is the Crew Clerk, "Kerroway?" "Yeah."
"Kerroway it's gonna be the Sherman Local at 7 AM this
morning." "Sherman Local right." "Out of Bayshore,
you know the way?" "Yeah." "You had that same job
last Sunday —— Okay Keroway-y-y-y-y." And we mutu-
ally hang up and I say to myself okay it's the Bayshore
bloody old dirty hagglous old coveted old madman
Sherman who hates me so much especially when we
were at Redwood Junction kicking boxcars and he always insists I work the rear end tho as one-year man
it would be easier for me to follow pot but I work rear
and he wants me to be right there with a block of wood
when a car or cut of cars kicked stops, so they wont roll
down that incline and start catastrophes, O well anyway
I'll be learning eventually to like the railroad and Sherman will like me some day, and anyway another day another dollar.

And there's my room, small, gray in the Sunday
morning, now all the franticness of the street and night
before is done with, bums sleep, maybe one or two
sprawled on sidewalk with empty poorboy on a sill ——
my mind whirls with life.

SO THERE I AM IN DAWN in my dim cell —— 2½
hours to go till the time I have to stick my railroad watch
in my jean watchpocket and cut out allowing myself ex-

actly 8 minutes to the station and the 7:15 train No. 112
I have to catch for the ride five miles to Bayshore
through four tunnels, emerging from the sad Rath scene
of Frisco gloom gleak in the rainymouth fogmorning
to a sudden valley with grim hills rising to the sea, bay
on left, the fog rolling in like demented in the draws
that have little white cottages disposed real-estatically
for come-Christmas blue sad lights —— my whole soul
and concomitant eyes looking out on this reality of living
and working in San Francisco with that pleased semi-
loin-located shudder, energy for sex changing to pain
at the portals of work and culture and natural foggy
fear.—— There I am in my little room wondering how
I'll really manage to fool myself into feeling that these
next 2½ hours will be well filled, fed, with work and
pleasure thoughts.—— It's so thrilling to feel the cold-
ness of the morning wrap around my thickquilt blankets
as I lay there, watch facing and ticking me, legs spread
in comfy skidrow soft sheets with soft tears or sew lines
in 'em, huddled in my own skin and rich and not spending a cent on —— I look at my littlebook —— and I stare
at the words of the Bible.—— On the floor I find last
red afternoon Saturday's *Chronicle* sports page with
news of football games in Great America the end of
which I bleakly see in the gray light entering.—— The
fact that Frisco is built of wood satisfies me in my peace,
I know nobody'll disturb me for 2½ hours and all bums
are asleep in their own bed of eternity awake or not,
bottle or not —— it's the joy I feel that counts for me.
—— On the floor's my shoes, big lumberboot flopjack
workshoes to colomp over rockbed with and not turn
the ankle —— solidity shoes that when you put them
on, yokewise, you know you're working now and so for
same reason shoes not be worn for any reason like joys
of restaurant and shows.—— Night-before shoes are on
the floor beside the clunkershoes a pair of blue canvas

shoes à la 1952 style, in them I'd trod soft as ghost the
indented hill sidewalks of Ah Me Frisco all in the glitter
night, from the top of Russian Hill I'd looked down
at one point on all roofs of North Beach and the Mexican nightclub neons, I'd descended to them on the old
steps of Broadway under which they were newly labor-
ing a mountain tunnel —— shoes fit for watersides, em-
barcaderos, hill and plot lawns of park and tiptop vista.
—— Workshoes covered with dust and some oil of engines —— the crumpled jeans nearby, belt, blue railroad
hank, knife, comb, keys, switch keys and caboose coach
key, the knees white from Pajaro Riverbottom finedusts,
the ass black from slick sandboxes in yardgoat after
yardgoat —— the gray workshorts, the dirty undershirt,
sad shorts, tortured socks of my life.—— And the Bible
on my desk next to the peanut butter, the lettuce, the
raisin bread, the crack in the plaster, the stiff-with-old-
dust lace drape now no longer laceable but hard as ——
after all those years of hard dust eternity in that Cameo
skid inn with red eyes of rheumy oldmen dying there
staring without hope out on the dead wall you can hardly
see thru windowdusts and all you heard lately in the
shaft of the rooftop middle way was the cries of a Chinese child whose father and mother were always telling
him to shush and then screaming at him, he was a pest
and his tears from China were most persistent and
worldwide and represented all our feelings in brokendown Cameo tho this was not admitted by bum one except for an occasional harsh clearing of throat in the halls
or moan of nightmarer —— by things like this and neg-
lect of a hard-eyed alcoholic oldtime chorusgirl maid
the curtains had now absorbed all the iron they could
take and hung stiff and even the dust in them was iron,
if you shook them they'd crack and fall in tatters to the
floor and spatter like wings of iron on the bong and the
dust would fly into your nose like filings of steel and

choke you to death, so I never touched them. My little room at 6 in the comfy dawn (at 4:30) and before me all that time, that fresh-eyed time for a little coffee to boil water on my hot plate, throw some coffee in, stir it, French style, slowly carefully pour it in my white tin cup, throw sugar in (not California beet sugar like I should have been using but New Orleans cane sugar, because beet racks I carried from Oakland out to Watson-ville many's the time, a 80-car freight train with noth-ing but gondolas loaded with sad beets looking like the heads of decapitated women).—— Ah me how but it was a hell and now I had the whole thing to myself, and make my raisin toast by sitting it on a little wire I'd especially bent to place over the hotplate, the toast crackled up, there, I spread the margarine on the still red hot toast and it too would crackle and sink in golden, among burnt raisins and this was my toast.—— Then two eggs gently slowly fried in soft margarine in my little skidrow frying pan about half as thick as a dime in fact less, a little piece of tiny tin you could bring on a camp trip —— the eggs slowly fluffled in there and swelled from butter steams and I threw garlic salt on them, and when they were ready the yellow of them had been slightly filmed with a cooked white at the top from the tin cover I'd put over the frying pan, so now they were ready, and out they came, I spread them out on top of my already prepared potatoes which had been boiled in small pieces and then mixed with the bacon I'd already fried in small pieces, kind of raggely mashed bacon potatoes, with eggs on top steaming, and on the side lettuce, with peanut butter dab nearby on side.—— I had heard that peanut butter and lettuce contained all the vitamins you should want, this after I had originally started to eat this combination because of the delicious-ness and nostalgia of the taste —— my breakfast ready at about 6:45 and as I eat already I'm dressing to go piece by piece and by the time the last dish is washed in the little sink at the boiling hotwater tap and I'm taking my lastquick slug of coffee and quickly rinsing the cup in the hot water spout and rushing to dry it and plop it in its place by the hot plate and the brown carton in which all the groceries sit tightly wrapped in brown paper, I'm already picking up my brakeman's lantern from where it's been hanging on the door handle and my tattered timetable's long been in my backpocket folded and ready to go, everything tight, keys, timetable, lantern, knife, handkerchief, wallet, comb, railroad keys, change and myself. I put the light out on the sad dab mad grub little diving room and hustle out into the fog of the flow, descending the creak hall steps where the old men are not yet sitting with Sunday morn papers because still asleep or some of them I can now as I leave hear beginning to disfawdle to wake in their rooms with their moans and yorks and scrapings and horror sounds, I'm going down the steps to work, glance to check time of watch with clerk cage clock.—— A hardy two or three oldtimers sitting already in the dark brown lobby under the tockboom clock, toothless, or grim, or elegantly mustached —— what thought in the world swirling in them as they see the young eager brakeman bum hurrying to his thirty dollars of the Sunday —— what memories of old homesteads, built without sympathy, hornyhanded fate dealt them the loss of wives, childs, moons —— libraries collapsed in their time —— oldtimers of the telegraph wired wood Frisco in the fog gray top time sitting in their brown sunk sea and will be there when this afternoon my face flushed from the sun, which at eight'll flame out and make sunbaths for us at Redwood, they'll still be here the color of paste in the green underworld and still reading the same editorial over again and wont understand where I've been or what for or what.—— I have to get out of there or suffocate, out of Third Street or become a worm, it's alright to live and bed-wine in and play the radio and cook little breakfasts and rest in but O my I've got to go now to work, I hurry down Third to Townsend for my 7:15 train —— it's 3 minutes to go, I start in a panic to jog, goddam it I didnt give myself enough time this morning, I hurry down under the Harrison ramp to the Oakland-Bay Bridge, down past Schweibacker-Frey the great dim red neon printshop always spectrally my father the dead executive I see there, I run and hurry past the beat Negro grocery stores where I buy all my peanut butter and raisin bread, past the redbrick railroad alley now mist and wet, across Townsend, the train is leaving!

FATUOUS RAILROAD MEN, the conductor old John J. Coppertwang 35 years pure service on ye olde S.P. is there in the gray Sunday morning with his gold watch out peering at it, he's standing by the engine yelling up pleasantries at old hoghead Jones and young fireman Smith with the baseball cap is at the fireman's seat munching sandwich —— "We'll how'd ye like old Johnny O yestiddy, I guess he didnt score so many touchdowns like we thought." "Smith bet six dollars on the pool down in Watsonville and said he's rakin' in thirty four." "I've been in that Watsonville pool ——." They've been in the pool of life fleartiming with one another, all the long pokerplaying nights in brownwood railroad places, you can smell the mashed cigar in the wood, the spittoon's been there for more than 750,099 yars and the dog's been in and out and these old boys by old shaded brown light have bent and muttered and young boys too with their new brakeman passenger uniform the tie undone the coat thrown back the flashing youth smile of happy fatuous well-fed goodjobbed careered futured pensioned hospitalized taken-care-of rail-road men.—— 35, 40 years of it and then they get to be conductors and in the middle of the night they've been for years called by the Crew Clerk yelling "Cassady? It's the Maximush localized week do you for the right lead" but now as old men all they have is a regular job, a regular train, conductor of the 112 with goldwatch is helling up his pleasantries at all fire dog crazy Satan hoghead Willis why the wildest man this side of France and Frankincense, he was known once to take his engine up that steep grade . . . 7:15, time to pull, as I'm running thru the station hearing the bell jangling and the steam chuff they're pulling out, O I come flying out on the platform and forget momentarily or that is never did know what track it was and whirl in confusion a while wondering what track and cant see no train and this is the time I lose there, 5, 6, 7 seconds when the train tho underway is only slowly upchugging to go and a man a fat executive could easily run up and grab it but when I yell to Assistant Stationmaster "Where's 112?" and he tells me the last track which is the track I never dreamed I run to it fast as I can go and dodge people à la Columbia halfback and cut into track fast as off-tackle where you carry the ball with you to the left and feint with neck and head and push of ball as tho you're gonna throw yourself all out to fly around that left end and everybody psychologically chuffs with you that way and suddenly you contract and you like whiff of smoke are buried in the hole in tackle, cutback play, you're flying into the hole almost before you yourself know it, flying into the track I am and there's the train about 30 yards away even as I look picking up tremendously momentum the kind of momentum I would have been able to catch if I'd a looked a second earlier —— but I run, I know I can catch it. Standing on the back platform are the rear brakeman and an old deadheading conductor ole Charley W. Jones, why he had seven wives and six kids and one time out at Lick no I guess it was Coyote he couldnt see on account of the steam and out he come and found his lantern in the igloo regular anglecock of my herald and they gave him fifteen benefits so now there he is in the Sunday har har owlala morning and he and young rear man watch incredulously his student brakeman running like a crazy trackman after their departing train. I feel like yelling "Make your airtest now make your airtest now!" knowing that when a passenger pulls out just about at the first crossing east of the station they pull the air a little bit to test the brakes, on signal from the engine, and this momentarily slows up the train and I could manage it, and could catch it, but they're not making no airtest the bastards, and I hek knowing I'm going to have to run like a sonofabitch. But suddenly I get embarrassed thinking what are all the people of the world gonna say to see a man running so devilishly fast with all his might sprinting thru life like Jesse Owens just to catch a goddam train and all of them with their hysteria wondering if I'll get killed when I catch the back platform and blam, I fall down and go boom and lay supine across the crossing, so the old flagman when the train has flowed by will see that everything lies on the earth in the same stew, all of us angels will die and we dont ever know how or our own diamond, O heaven will enlighten us and open you eyes —— open our eyes, open our eyes.—— I know I wont get hurt, I trust my shoes, hand grip, feet, solidity of yipe and cripe of gripe and grip and strength and need no mystic strength to measure the musculature in my rib rack —— but damn it all it's a social embarrassment to be caught sprinting like a maniac after a train especially with two men gaping at me from rear of train and shaking their heads and yelling I cant make

it even as I halfheartedly sprint after them with open
eyes trying to communicate that I can and not for them
to get hysterical or laugh, but I realize it's all too much
for me, not the run, not the speed of the train which
anyway two seconds after I gave up the complicated
chase did indeed slow down at the crossing in the airtest before chugging up again for good and Bayshore.
So I was late for work, and old Sherman hated me and
was about to hate me more.

THE GROUND I WOULD HAVE EATEN in
solitude, cronch —— the railroad earth, the flat stretches
of long Bayshore that I have to negotiate to get to
Sherman's bloody caboose on track 17 ready to go
with pot pointed to Redwood and the morning's 3-hour
work.—— I get off the bus at Bayshore Highway
and rush down the little street and turn in —— boys
riding the pot of a switcheroo in the yardgoat day come
yelling by at me from the headboards and footboards
"Come on down ride with us" otherwise I would have
been about 3 minutes even later to my work but now
I hop on the little engine that momentarily slows up
to pick me up and it's alone not pulling anything but
tender, the guys have been up to the other end of the
yard to get back on some track of necessity.—— That boy
will have to learn to flag himself without nobody help-
ing him as many's the time I've seen some of these
young goats think they have everything but the plan
is late, the word will have to wait, the massive arboreal
thief with the crime of the kind, and air and all kinds
of ghouls   ZONKed! made tremendous by the flare
of the whole crime and encrudalatures of all kinds ——
San Franciscos and shroudband Bayshores the last and
the last furbelow of the eek plot pall prime tit top work
oil twicks and wouldn't you? —— the railroad earth I

would have eaten alone, cronch, on foot head bent to
get to Sherman who ticking watch observes with finicky
eyes the time to go to give the hiball sign get on going
it's Sunday no time to waste the only day of his long
seven-day-a-week worklife he gets a chance to rest a
little bit at home when "Eee Christ" when "Tell that
sonofabitch student this is no party picnic damn this
shit and throb tit you tell them something and how do
you what the hell expect to underdries out tit all you
bright tremendous trouble anyway, we's LATE" and
this is the way I come rushing up late. Old Sherman is
sitting in the crummy over his switch lists, when he sees
me with cold blue eyes he says "You know you're supposed to be here 7:30 dont you so what the hell you
doing gettin' in here at 7:50 you're twenty goddam
minutes late, what the fuck you think this your birth-
day?" and he gets up and leans off the rear bleak platform and gives the high sign to the enginemen up front
we have a cut of about 12 cars and they say it easy and
off we go slowly at first, picking up momentum to the
work, "Light that goddam fire" says Sherman he's wearing brandnew workshoes just about bought yestiddy and
I notice his clean coveralls that his wife washed and set
on his chair just that morning probably and I rush up
and throw coal in the potbelly flop and take a fusee
and two fusees and light them crack em. Ah fourth of
the July when the angels would smile on the horizon
and all the racks where the mad are lost are returned
to us forever from Lowell of my soul prime and single
meditated longsong hope to heaven of prayers and
angels and of course the sleep and interested eye of images and but now we detect the missing buffoon there's
the poor goodman rear man aint even on the train yet
and Sherman looks out sulkily the back door and sees
his rear man waving from fifteen yards aways to stop
and wait for him and being an old railroad man he cer-

tainly isnt going to run or even walk fast, it's well understood, conductor Sherman's got to get up off his switch-
list desk chair and pull the air and stop the goddam
train for rear man Arkansaw Charley, who sees this
done and just come up lopin' in his flop overalls without no care, so he was late too, or at least had gone
gossiping in the yard office while waiting for the stupid
head brakeman, the tagman's up in front on the pre-
sumably pot. "First thing we do is pick up a car in front
at Redwood so all's you do get off at the crossing and
stand back to flag, not too far." "Dont I work the head
end?" "You work the hind end we got not much to do
and I wanna get it done fast," snarls the conductor.
"Just take it easy and do what we say and watch and
flag." So it's peaceful Sunday morning in California and
off we go, tack-a-tick, lao-tichi-couch, out of the Bayshore yards, pause momentarily at the main line for
the green, ole 71 or ole whatever been by and now we
get out and go swamming up the tree valleys and town
vale hollows and main street crossing parking-lot last-
night attendant plots and Stanford lots of the world —
to our destination in the Pooh which I can see, and, so
to while the time I'm up in the cupolo and with my
newspaper dig the latest news on the front page and
also consider and make notations of the money I spent
already for this day Sunday absolutely not jot spend
a nothing — California rushes by and with sad eyes
we watch it reel the whole bay and the discourse falling off to gradual gils that ease and graduate to Santa
Clara Valley then and the fig and behind is the fog im-
memoriate while the mist closes and we come running
out to the bright sun of the Sabbath Californiay —

At Redwood I get off and standing on sad oily ties
of the brakie railroad earth with red flag and torpedoes
attached and fusees in backpocket with timetable crushed
against and I leave my hot jacket in crummy standing

there then with sleeves rolled up and there's the porch of a Negro home, the brothers are sitting in shirtsleeves talking with cigarettes and laughing and little daughter standing amongst the weeds of the garden with her playpail and pigtails and we the railroad men with soft signs and no sound pick up our flower, according to same goodman train order that for the last entire lifetime of attentions ole conductor industrial worker harlotized Sherman has been reading carefully son so's not to make a mistake:

"Sunday morning October 15 pick up flower car at Redwood, Dispatcher M.M.S."

I'D PUT A BLOCK OF WOOD under the wheels of the car and watch it writhe and crack as the car eased up on it and stopped and sometimes didnt at all but just rolled on leaving the wood flattened to the level of the rail with upthrusted crackee ends.—Afternoons in Lowell long ago I'd wondered what the grimy men were doing with big boxcars and blocks of wood in their hands and when far above the ramps and rooftops of the great gray warehouse of eternity I'd see the immortal canal clouds of redbrick time, the drowse so heavy in the whole July city it would hang even in the dank gloom of my father's shop outside where they kept big rolltrucks with little wheels and flat silvery platforms and junk in corners and boards, the ink dyed into the oily wood as deep as a black river folded therein forever, contrasts for the whitepuff cream-clouds outdoors that you just can see standing in the dust moted hall door over the old 1830 Lowell Dickens redbrick floating like in an old cartoon with little bird designs floating by too, all of a gray daguerrotype mystery in the whorly spermy waters of the canal.—— Thus in the same way the afternoons in the S.P. redbrick alley, remembering my wonder at the slow grinding movement and squee of gigantic boxcars and flats and gons rolling by with that overpowering steel dust crenching closh and clack of steel on steel, the shudder of the whole steely proposition, a car going by with a brake on and so the whole brakebar —— *monstre empoudrement de fer en enfer* the frightening fog nights in California when you can see thru the mist the monsters slowly passing and hear the whee whee squee, those merciless wheels that one time Conductor Ray Miles on my student trips said, "When those wheels go over your leg they dont care about you" same way with that wood that I sacrifice.—— What those grimy men had been doing some of em standing on top of the boxcars and signalling far down the redbrick canal alleys of Lowell and some old men slowly like bums moving around over rails with nothing to do, the big cut of cars squeeing by with that teethgritting cree cree and gigantic hugsteel bending rails into earth and making ties move, now I knew from working as on the Sherman Local on Sundays we dealt with blocks of wood because of an incline in the ground that made kicked cars keep going and you had to ride them brake them and stop them up with blocks. Lessons I learned there, like, "Put, tie a good brake on him, we dont want to start chasin the sonofabitch back to the City when we kick a car again him," okay, but I'm playing the safety rules of the safety book to the T and so now here I am the rear man on the Sherman Local, we've set out our Sunday morning preacher blossom flower car and made curtsies bows to the sabbath God in the dark everything has been arranged in that fashion and according to old traditions reaching back to Sutter's Mill and the times when the pioneers sick of hanging around the hardware store all week had put on their best vestments and smoked and jaw-bleaked in front of the wooden church and old railroad men of the 19th century the inconceivably ancient S.P. of another era with stovepipe hats and flowers in their lapels and had made the moves with the few cars into the goldtown milkbottle with the formality and the different chew the thinky thought,—— They give the sign and kick a car, with wood in hand I run out, the old conductor yells "You'd better brake him he's going too fast can you get im?" "Okay" and I run and take it easy on a jog and wait and here's the big car looming over me has just switched into its track from the locomotive tracks where (the lead) all the angling and arrowing's been done by the conductor who throws the switch, reads the taglist, throws the switch —— so up the rungs I go and according to safety rules with one hand I hang on, with the other I brake, slowly, according to a joint, easing up, till I reach the cut of cars waiting and into it gently my braked boxcar bangs, zommm —— vibrations, things inside shake, the cradle rockababy merchandise zomms with it, all the cars at this impact go forward about a foot and crush woodblocks earlier placed, I jump down and place a block of wood and just neatly glue it under the steel lip of that monstrous wheel and everything stops. And so I turn back to take care of the next kicked car which is going down the other track and also quite fast, I jog, finding wood en route, run up the rung, stop it, safety rule hanging on one hand forgetting the conductor's "Tie a good brake on it," something I should have learned then as a year later in Guadaloupe hundreds of miles down the line I tied poor brakes on three flats, the flat handbrakes that have old rust and loose chains, poorly with one hand safety wise hanging on in case unexpected joint would jolt me off and under merciless wheels whose action with blocks of wood my bones would belie —— bam, at Guadaloupe they kicked a cut of cars against my poorly braked flats and everything began parading down the incline back to San Luis Obispo, if it hadn't been for the alert old conductor looking out of the crummy switch lists to see this parade and running out to throw switches in front of it and unlocking switch locks as fast as the cars kept coming, a kind of comic circus act with him in floppy clown pants and hysterical horror darting from switch stand to switch stand and the guys in back hollering, the pot taking off after the cut and catching it almost pushing it but the couplers closing just in time and the engine braking everything to a stop, 30 feet almost in front of the final derail which the old winded conductor couldnt have finally made, we'd all have lost our jobs, my safety rule brakes had not taken momentum of steel and slight land inclines into consideration ... if it had been Sherman at Guadaloupe I would have been hated Keoroowaaayy.

GUADALOUPE IS 275.5 miles down the shining rail from San Francisco, down on the subdivision named after it, the Guadaloupe — the whole Coast Division begins at those sad dead end blocks of Third and Townsend where grass grows from soot beds like green hair of old tokay heroes long slanted into the ground like the railroad men of the 19th century whom I saw in the Colorado plains at little train order stations slanted into the ground of the hard dry dustcake, boxed, mawklipped, puking grit, fondled by the cricket, gone aslant so far sunk gravewise boxdeep into the foot of the sole of the earth Oh, you'd think they had never suffered and dropped real sweats to that unhumped earth, had never voiced juicy sorrow words from blackcaked lips now make no more noise than the tire of an old tin lizzy the tin of which is zinging in the sun winds this afternoon, ah spectral Cheyenne Wellses and train order

Denver Rio Grandes Northern Pacifics and Atlantic
Coast Lines and Wunposts of America, all gone.—— The
Coast Division of the ole S.P. which was built in umpteen
o too too and used to run a little crazy crooked mainline
up and down the hills of Bayshore like a crazy cross
country track for European runners, this was their gold
carrying bandito held up railroad of the old Zorro night
of inks and furly caped riders.—— But now 'tis the modern ole Coast Division S.P. and begins at those dead
end blocks and at 4:30 the frantic Market Street and
Sansome Street commuters as I say come hysterically
running for their 112 to get home on time for the 5:30
televisions Howdy Doody of their gun toting Neal Cassady'd Hopalong childrens. 1.9 miles to 23rd Street,
another 1.2 Newcomb, another 1.0 to Paul Avenue
and etcetera these being the little piss stops on that 5
miles short run thru 4 tunnels to mighty Bayshore,
Bayshore at milepost 5.2 shows you as I say that gigantic valley wall sloping in with sometimes in extinct
winter dusks the huge fogs milking furling meerolling
in without a sound but as if you could hear the radar
hum, the oldfashioned dullmasks mouth of Potato Patch
Jack London old scrollwaves crawling in across the gray
bleak North Pacific with a wild fleck, a fish, the wall of
a cabin, the old arranged wallworks of a sunken ship,
the fish swimming in the pelvic bones of old lovers lay
tangled at the bottom of the sea like slugs no longer dis-
cernible bone by bone but melted into one squid of time,
that fog, that terrible and bleak Seattleish fog that po-
tatopatch wise comes bringing messages from Alaska
and from the Aleutian mongol, and from the seal, and
from the wave, and from the smiling porpoise, that fog
at Bayshore you can see waving in and filling in rills and
rolling down and making milk on hillsides and you
think, "It's hypocrisy of men makes these hills grim."
—— To the left at the Bayshore mountain wall there's

all your San Fran Bay pointing across the broadflat
blues to the Oakland lostness and the train the mainline
train runs and clack and clackity clicks and makes the
little Bayshore yard office a passing fancy things so important to the railroad men the little yellowish shack of
clerks and paper onion skin train order lips and clear-
ances of conductors and waybills tacked and typed and
stamped from Kearney Neb. on in with mooing cows
that have moved over 3 different railroads and all ye
such facts, that passed in a flash and the train negotiates,
on, passing Visitacion Tower, that by old Okie railroad
men of now-California aint at all mexicanized in pro-
nunciation, Vi Zi Tah Sioh, but is simply called, Visitation, like on Sunday morning, and oft you hear, "Visitation Tower, Visitation Tower," ah ah ah ah aha.——
Mile post 6.9, the following 8.6 Butler Road far from
being a mystery to me by the time I became a brakeman
was the great sad scene of yard clerking nights when at
the far end of a 80 car freight the numbers of which with
my little lamp I was taking down as I crunched over
the gravel and all backtired, measuring how far I had to
go by the sad streetlamp of Butler Road shining up
ahead at the wall's end of long black sadmouth longcars
of ye iron reddark railroad night—with stars above,
and the smashby Zipper and the fragrance of locomotive
coalsmoke as I stand aside and let them pass and far
down the line at night around that South San Fran airport you can see that sonofabitch red light waving Mars
signal light waving in the dark big red markers blowing
up and down and sending fires in the keenpure lostpurity
lovelyskies of old California in the late sad night of
autumn spring comefall winter's summertime tall, like
trees.—— all of it, and Butler Road no mystery to me,
no blind spot in this song, but well known, I could also
measure how far I had to go by the end of the gigantic
rose neon six miles long you'd think saying WEST

COAST BETHLEHEM STEEL as I'd be taking down the numbers of boxcars JC 74635 (Jersey Central) D&RG 38376 and NYC and PR and all the others, my work almost done when that huge neon was even with me and at the same time this meant the sad little streetlamp of Butler Road was only 50 feet away and no cars beyond that because that was the crossing where they'd cut them and then fold them over into another track of the South City yards, things of brake significance switch significance I only got to learn later. —— So SF milepost 9.3 and what a bleak little main street, o my goodness, the fog'd roll in fine from there and the little neon cocktails with a little cherry on a toothpick and the bleak foglike green Chronicles in 10¢ sidewalk tin clonks, and yr bars with fat slick haired ex troopers inside drinking and October in the poolhall and all, where I'd go for a few bars of candy or desultory soups between chores as yardclerk when I was a yardclerk digging the lostness on that side, the human, and then having to go to the other end, a mile towards the Bay, to the great Armour & Swift slaughterplants where I'd take down the numbers of meat reefers and sometimes have to step aside and wait while the local came in and did some switching and the tagman or conductor would always tell me which ones were staying, which ones going.—— Always at night, and always soft ground of like manure but really rat ground underneath, the countless rats I saw and threw rocks at till I felt like being sick, I'd hurry fleeing as from nightmare from that hole and sometimes fabricated phoney numbers instead of going too near a gigantic woodpile which was so full of rats it was like their tenement.—— And the sad cows mooing inside where little ratty Mexicans and Californians with bleak unpleasant unfriendly faces and going-to-work jalopies were milling around in their bloody work —— till finally I worked it on a Sunday, the Armour & Swift yards, and saw that the Bay was 60 feet away and I'd never known it, but a dump yard a recka of crap and rat havens worse than ever tho beyond it the waters did ripple bluely and did in the sad morning clarity show clear flat mirrors clear to Oakland and the Alameda places across the way.—— And in the hard wind of the Sunday morning I heard the mutter of the tinware walls of brokendown abandoned slaughter house warehouses, the crap inside and dead rats killed by that local on off nights and some even I might have hit with my jacketful of protective rocks, but mostly systematically killed rats laying around in the keen heartbreaking cloud haunted wildwind day with big silver airplanes of civilized hope taking off across the stinking swamp and filthy tin flats for places in the air. —— Gah, bah, ieoeoeoeoe —— it has a horrible filthy moaning sound you'd hear eiderdowning in that flydung those hideaway silos and murdered tinpaint aisles, scum, of salt, and bah oh bah and harbors of the rat, the axe, the sledgehammer, the moo cows and all that, one big South San Francisco horror there's your milepost 9.3. —— After that the rushing train takes you to San Bruno clear and far around a long bend circling the marsh of the SSF airport and then on in to Lomita Park milepost 12.1 where the sweet commuter trees are and the redwoods crash and talk about you when you pass in the engine the boilers of which redly cast your omnipotent shadow out on the night.—— You see all the lil ranchstyle California homes and in the evening people sipping in livingrooms open to the sweetness, the stars, the hope that lil children must see when they lay in little beds and bedtime and look up and a star throbs for them above the railroad earth, and the train calls, and they think tonite the stars will be out, they come, they leave, they lave, they angelicize, ah me, I must come from a land where they let the children cry, ah me

I wish I was a child in California when the sun's gone down and the Zipper crashes by and I could see thru the redwood or the fig tree my throbbing hope-light shining just for me and making milk on Permanente hillsides horrible Kafka cement factories or no, rats of South City slaughterhouses or no, no, or no, I wish I was a little child in a crib in a little ranchstyle sweet house with my parents sipping in the livingroom with their picture window pointing out on the little backyard of lawning chairs and the fence, the ranchstyle brown pointed full fence, the stars above, the pure dry golden smelling night, and just beyond a few weeds, and blocks of wood, and rubber tires, bam the main line of the Ole SP and the train flashing by, toom, tboom, the great crash of the black engine, the grimy red men inside, the tender, then the long snake freighttrain and all the numbers and all the whole thing flashing by, gcrachs, thunder, the world is going by all of it finally terminated by the sweet little caboose with its brown smoky light inside where old conductor bends over waybills and up in the cupolo the rear man sits looking out once in a while and saying to himself all black, and the rear markers, red, the lamps in the caboose rear porch, and the thing all gone howling around the bend to Burlingame to Mountain View to the sweet San Joses of the night the further down Gilroys Carnaderos Corporals and that bird of Chittenden of the dawn, your Logans of the strange night all be-lit and insected and mad, your Watsonvilles sea marshes your long long line and mainline track sticky to the touch in the midnight star.

MILE POST 46.9 is San Jose scene of a hundred interested bums lounging in the weeds along the track with their packs of junk, their buddies, their private water-

64

tanks, their cans of water to make coffee or tea or soup with, and their bottle of tokay wine or usually muskatel. —— The Muskat California is all around them, in the sky blue, tatteredly white clouds are being shoved across the top of the Santa Clara Valley from Bayshore where a high fogwind came and thru South City gaps too and the peace lies heavy in the sheltered valley where the bums have found a temporary rest.—— Hot drowse in the dry weeds, just hollows of dry reed stick up and you walk against them crashing.—— "Well boy, how's about a shot of rum to Watsonville." "This aint rum boy, this is a new kinda shit" —— a colored hobo sitting on a shitty old newspaper of last year and's been used by Rat Eye Jim of the Denver viaducts who came thru here last spring with a package of dates on his back —— "Things aint been as bad as this since 1906!" Now it's 1952 October and the dew is on the grain of this real ground. One of the boys picks up a piece of tin from the ground (that got bounced off a gon in a sudden sprrram of freights ramming together in the yard from the bucklin slack) (bowm!) —— pieces of tin go flying off, fall in the weeds, outside track No. 1.—— The hobo puts the tin on rocks over the fire and uses it to toast some bread but's drinking tokay and talking to the other boys and toast burns just like in tile kitchen tragedies.—— The bum comes curses angrily because he lost some bread, and kicks a rock, and says "Twenty eight years I spent inside the walls of Dannemora and I had my fill of excitin panoramas of the great actions like when drunken Canneman wrote me that letter fum minneapoly and it was jess about chicago sponges —— I turd him looka jock you caint —— well I wrote im a letter ennyways." Aint been a soul listening because no one listens to a bum all the other bums are blagdengabsting and you cant find nor finangilate yr way out of that —— all talking at the same time and all of them confused. You have to go back to the railroad man to understand.—— Like, say, you ask a man "Where's track 109?" —— nu —— if it's a bum he'll say "Cart right over there dadday, and see if the old boy in the blue bandana knows, I'm Slim Holmes Hubbard from Ruston Louisiana and I got no time and got no knowledge to make me ways of knowin what where that track 109—only thing's I got, is —— I want a dime, if you can spare a dime I'll go along my way peacefully —— if you cant I'll go along my way peacefully —— ya cant win —— ya cant lose —— and from between here to Bismarck Idaho I got nothing but lost and lost and lost everything I ever had." You've got to admit these bums into your soul when they talk like that —— most of them rasp "Track 109 Chillicothe Ioway" thru the stubbles and spits of their beard —— and wander off dragassing packs so huge, profound, heavy —— dismembered bodies are in there you'd think —— red eyes, wild wild hair, the railroad men look at them with amazement and at first sight then never look again —— what would wives say?—— If you ask a railroad man what track is 109, he stop, stop chewing his gum, shift his package his coatlamp or lunch and turn, and spit, and squint at the mountains to the east and roll his eyes very slowly in the private cavern of his eyebone between brow bone and cheek bone, and say, still deliberating and having deliberated "They call it track 109 but they should call it 110, it's right next to the ice platform you know the icehouse up there ——" "Yeah ——" "There it is, from track one on the main line here we start the numbers but the ice house make em jump they make a turn and you have to go across track 110 to get to 109 —— But you never have to go to 109 too often —— so it's just like 109 was jess missing from the yard ...numbers, see..." "Yeah" —— I know it for sure —— "I know it for sure now." "And there she is ——" "Thanks —— I gotta get there fast" —— "That's the

trouble with the railroad, you always gotta get there fast
—— 'cause if you dont it's like turning down a local on
the phone and say you want to turn over and go to
sleep (like Mike Ryan did last Monday)" he's sayin to
himself.—— And we walk wave and are gone.

This is the cricket in the reed. I sat down in the
Pajaro riverbottoms and lit fires and slept with my coat
on top of my brakeman's lantern and considered the
California life staring at the blue sky ——

The conductor is in there hanging around waiting
for his train orders —— when he gets them he'll give the
engineer the hiball sign, a little side to side wave of the
palmed hand, and off we go —— the old hoghead gives
orders for steam, the young fireman complies, the hoghead kicks and pulls at his big lever throttle and sometimes jumps up to wrestle with it like hugely an angel
in hell and pulls the whistle twice toot toot we're leaving, and you hear the first chug of the engine —— chug
—— a failure like —— chug a lut —— zoom —— chug
CHUG —— the first movement —— the train's underway.——

SAN JOSE —— because the soul of the railroad is the
chain gang run, the long freight train you see snaking
down the track with a puff puff en jyne pulling is the
traveler the winner the arterial moody mainline maker
of the rail —— San Jose is 50 miles south of Frisco and
is the center of the Coast Division chain gang or long
road run activity, known as the horn because the pivot
point for rails going down from Frisco toward Santa
Barbara and L.A. and rails going and shining back to
Oakland via Newark and Niles on sub lines that also
cross the mighty main line of the Fresno bound Valley
Division.—— San Jose is where I should have been living
instead of Third Street Frisco, for these reasons: 4 o'clock

in the morning, in San Jose, comes a call on the phone it is the Chief Dispatcher calling from 4th and Townsend in the Sad Frisco, "Keroowayyyy? it's deadhead on 112 to San Jose for a drag east with Conductor Degnan got that?" "Yeh deadahead 112 drag east right," meaning, go back to bed and rise again around 9, you're being paid all this time and boy dont worry about a durg and doo-gaddm things, at 9 all's you gotta do is get ups and you already done made how many dollars? anyways in your sleep and put on your gig clothes and cut out and take a little bus and go down to the San Jose yard office down by the airport there and in the yard office are hundreds of interested railroad men and tackings of tickers and telegraph and the engines are being lined up and num-bered and markered out there, and new engines keep rushing up from the roundhouse, & everywhere in the gray air tremendous excitements of movement of rolling stocks and the making of great wages.—— You go down there, find your conductor who'll just be some old baggy-pants circus comedian with a turned up hatbrim and red face and red handkerchief and grimy waybills and switchlists in his hand and far from carrying a student big brakeman lantern like you's got his little old 10 year old tiny lantern from some old boomer bought and the batteries of which he has to keep buying at Davegas instead of like the student getting free at the yard office, because after 20 years on the rr you gotta find some way to be different and also t'lighten the burdens you carry around with yourself, he's there, leaning, by spit-toons, with others, you go up hat over eyes, say "Con-ductor Degnan?" "I'm Degnan, well it doesnt look like anything'll bevore noon so just take it easy and be around" so you go into the blue room they call it, where blue flies buzz and hum around old zawful dirty couch tops stretched on benches with the stuffing coming out and attracting and probably breeding further flies, and there you lie down if it ain't already full of sleeping

brakemen and you turn your shoetops up to the dirty
old brown sad ceiling of time there, haunted by the clack
of telegraphs and the chug of engines outdoors enough
to make you go in your pants, and turns your hatbrim
over yr eyes, and go ahead and sleep.—— Since 4 in the
morning, since 6 in the morning when still the sleep was
on yr eyes in that dark dream house you've been getting
1.90 per hour and it is now 10 A M and the train aint
even made up and "not before noon" says Degnan so
that by noon you'll already have been working (because
counting from time of 112, deadhead time) six hours
and so you'll leave San Jose with your train around noon
or maybe further at one and not get to the terminal
great chaingang town of Watsonville where everything's going (L.A. ward) till 3 in the afternoon and
with happy mishaps 4 or 5, nightfall, when down there
waiting for the herder's sign enginemen and trainmen
see the long red sad sun of waning day falling on the
lovely old landmark milepost 98.2 farm and day's done,
run's done, they been being paid since down dawn of
that day and only traveled about 50 miles.—— This will
be so, so sleep in the blue room, dream of 1.90 per hour
and also of your dead father and your dead love and the
mouldering in your bones and the eventual Fall of you
—— the train wont be made up till noon and no one
wants to bother you *till* —— lucky child and railroad
angel softly in your steel propositioned sleep.

So much more to Jan Jose.

So if you
live in San Jose you have the advantage of 3 hours of
extra sleep at home not counting the further sleep on
the blue room rot puff leather couch —— nevertheless
I was using the 50 mile ride from 3rd Street as my library, bringing books and papers in a little tattered
black bag already 10 years old which I'd originally
bought on a pristine morning in Lowell in 1942 to go
to sea with, arriving in Greenland that summer, and so

a bag so bad a brakeman seeing me with it in the San Jose yard coffee shop said whooping loud "A railroad loot bag if I ever saw one!" and I didnt even smile or acknowledge and that was the beginning middle and extent of my social rapport on the railroad with the good old boys who worked it, thereafter becoming known as Kerouaayyy the Indian with the phony name and everytime we went by the Pomo Indians working sectionhand tracks, gandy dancers with greasy black hair I waved and smiled and was the only man on the S.P. who did so except old hogheads always do wave and smile and sectionhand bosses who are old white bespectacled respectable old toppers and topers of time and everybody respects, but the dark Indian and the eastern Negro, with sledgehammers and dirtypants to them I waved and shortly thereafter I read a book and found out that the Pomo Indian battle cry is Ya Ya Henna, which I thought once of yelling as the engine crashboomed by but what would I be starting but derailments of my own self and engineer.—— All the railroad opening up and vaster and vaster until finally when I did quit it a year later I saw it again but now over the waves of the sea, the entire Coast Division winding down along the dun walls of bleak headland balboa amerikay, from a ship, and so the railroad opens up on the waves that are Chinese and on the orient shroud and sea.—— It runs ragged to the plateau clouds and Pucalpas and lost Andean heights far below the world rim, it also bores a deep hole in the mind of man and freights a lot of interesting cargo in and out the holes precipitate and otherwise hidingplaces and imitative cauchemar of eternity, as you'll see.

SO ONE MORNING they called me at 3rd Street at about 4 A M and I took the early morning train to San

Jose, arriving there 7:30 was told not to worry about anything till about 10 so I went out in my inconceivably bum's existence went looking for pieces of wire that I could bend in such a way over my hotplate so they would support little raisin breads to make toast and also looking if possible for better than that a chickenwire arrangement on which I could sit pots to heat water and pans to fry eggs since the hotplate was so powerful it often burned and blackcaked the bottom of my eggs if by chance I'd overlook the possibility while busy peeling my potatoes or otherwise involved —— I'd walk around, San Jose had a junk yard across the track, I went in there and lookt around, stuff in there so useless the proprietor never came out, I who was earning 600 a month made off with a piece of chicken wire for my hotplate.—— Here it was 11 and still no train made up, gray, gloomy, wonderful day —— I wandered down the little street of cottages to the big boulevard of Jose and had Carnation ice cream and coffee in the morning, whole bevies and classrooms of girls came in with tight-fitting and sloosesucking sweaters and everything on earth on, it was some academy of dames suddenly come to gossip coffee and I was there in my baseball hat black slick oiled and rusted jacket weather jacket with fur collar that I had used to lean my head on in the sands of Watsonville riverbottoms and grits of Sunnyvale across from Westinghouse near Schukl's student days ground where my first great moment of the railroad had taken place over by Del Monte's when I kicked my first car and Whitey said "You're the boss do it pull the pin with a will put your hand in there and pull 'cause you're the boss" and it was October night, dark, clean, clear, dry, piles of leaves by the track in the sweet scented dark and beyond them crates of the Del Monte fruit and workers going around in crate wagons with under reaching stuckers and —— never will forget

Whitey saying that.—— By same reminiscence of doubt, in spite and because of, wanted to save all me money for Mexico, I also refused to spend 75 cents or even 35 cents less for a pair of workgloves, instead, after initial losing of my first bought workglove while setting out that sweet San Mateo flower car on Sunday morning with the Sherman local I resolved to get all my other gloves from the ground and so went for weeks with my black hand clutching sticky cold iron of engines in the dewy cold night, till I finally found the first glove outside the San Jose yard office, a brown cloth glove with red Mephistophelean lining, picking it up limp and damp from the ground and smashed it on my knee and let it dry and wore it.—— Final other glove found outside Watsonville yard office, a little leather imitation outside glove with inside warm lining and cut with scissors or razor at the wrist to facilitate putting it on and obviate yanking and yunking.—— These were my gloves, I'd lost as I say my first glove in San Mateo, the second with Conductor Degnan while waiting for the all clear signal from the pot (working rear because of his fear) by the track at Lick, the long curve, the traffic on 101 making it difficult to hear and in fact it was the old conductor who in the dark of that Saturday night did finally hear, I heard nothing, I ran to the caboose as it leapt ahead with the slack and got on counting my red lamps gloves fusees and whatnots and realizing with horror as the train pulled along I had dropped one of my gloves at Lick, damn! —— now I had two new gloves from off the ground pickied.—— At noon of that day the engine still wasnt on, the old hoghead hadnt left home yet where he'd picked up his kid on a sunny sidewalk with open arms and kissed him the late red john time of afternoon before, so I was there sleeping on the horrible old couch when by god in some way or other and after I'd gone out several times to check and

72

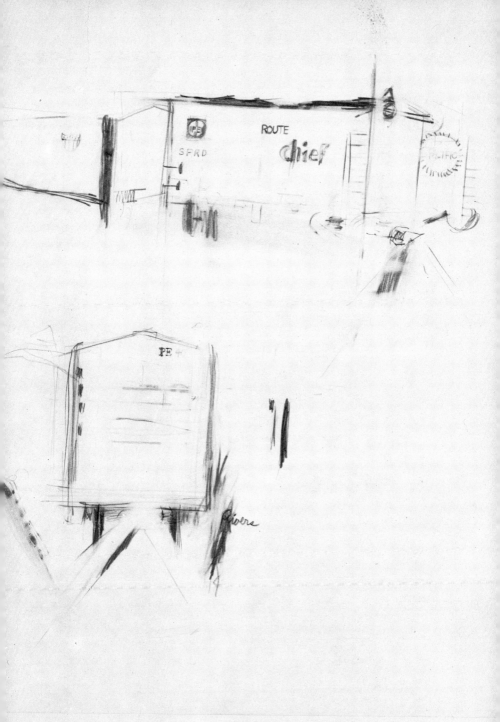

climb around the pot which was now tied on and the
conductor and rear man having coffee in the shop and
even the fireman and then I went back for further
musings or nappings on the seat cover expecting them
to call me, when in my dreams I hear a double toot toot
and hear a great anxiety engine taking off and it's my
engine but I dont realize it right away, I think it's some
slomming woeful old blacktrackpot whack cracking
along in a dream or dream reality when suddenly I
wake up to the fact they didnt know I was sleeping in
the blue room, and they got their orders, and gave the
hiball, and there they go to Watsonville leaving the head
man behind —— as tradition goes, fireman and engineer
if they dont see the head man on the engine and they've
gotten the sign, off they go, they have nothing to do
with these sleepy trainmen.—— I leap up grab lamp and
in the gray day and running precisely over the spot
where I'd found that brown glove with red lining and
thinking of it in the fury of my worry and as I dash I
see the engine way down the line 50 years picking up
and chufgffouffing and the whole train's rumbling after
and cars waiting at the crossing for the event, it's MY
TRAIN!—— Off I go loping and running fast over the
glove place, and over the road, and over the corner of
the junk field where I'd searched for tin also that lazy
morning, amazied mouth-gagaped railroad men about
five of them are watching this crazy student running
after his engine as it leaves for Watsonville —— is he
going to make it? Inside 30 seconds I was abreast with
the iron ladder and shifting lantern t'other hand to
grab holt of and get on and climb, and anyway the whole
shebang restopped again at a red to allow old I think 71
get through the station yards, it was I think by now
almost 3 o'clock I'd slept and earned or started to earn
incredible overtimes and this nightmare transpiring.——
So they got the red and stopped anyway and I had my

train made and sat on the sand box to catch my breath, no comment whatever in the world on the bleak jawbones and cold blue okie eyes of that engineer and fireman they must have been holding some protocol with the iron railroad in their hearts for all they cared about this softheaded kid who'd run down the cinders to his late lost work

Forgive me o Lord

AT THE RICKETY FENCEBACK Del Monte Fruitpacking Company which is directly across the track from the San Jose passenger station there is a curve in the track, a curve shmurve of eternity rememberable from the dreams of the railroad dark I had where I'm working unspeakable locals with Indians and suddenly we come upon a great Indian caucus in an underground subterraneana somewhere right there in the vicinity of the Del Monte curve (where Indians work anyway) (packing the crates, the cans, the fruit in cans with syrup) and I'm with the heroes of the Portuguese bars of San Francisco watching dances and hearing revolutionary speeches like the speeches of the revolutionary sod squat down heroes of Culiacan where by the bark of the wave in the drearylit drolling night I have heard them say *la tierra esta la notre* and knew they mean it and for this reason the dream of the Indians revolutionary meeting and celebrating in the bottom lip cellar of the railroad earth.—— The train goes around the curve there and gently I lean out of the grabiron darks and look and there's our little clearance and train order sitting in a piece of string which is stretched between the two train order bamrods, as the train passes the trainmen simply (usually the fireman) reaches out with whole arm so to make sure not to miss and hooks the string in passing (the string being taut) and off

74

comes the string and the two bows which are rigid sorta ping a little and in yr arm is looped the train orders on yellow onionskin tied by string, the engineer upon receipt of this freight takes the string and slowly according to years of personal habit in the manner of undoing train order strings undoes the string and then according again to habit unfolds the paper to read and sometimes they even put glasses on like great professors of ivy universities to read as that big engine goes chug chugging across and down the green land of California and Mexicans of railside mexshacks standing with eyes shaded watching us past, see the great bespectacled monk student in engineer of the night peering learnedly at his little slip in big grimy paw and it reads, date, "Oct 3 1952, Train Orders, to Train 2-9222, issued 2:04 PM, wait at Rucker till 3:58 for eastbound 914, do not go beyond Corporal till 4:08 and etc." all the various orders which the train order dispatchers and various thinking officials at switch towers and telephones are thinking up in the great metaphysical passage of iron traffics of the rail — we all take turns reading, like they say to young students "Read it carefully dont leave it up to us to decide if there are any mistakes many's the time a student found a mistake that the engineer and fireman out of years of habit didnt see so read it carefully" so I go over the whole thing reading even over and over again checking dates the time, like, the time of the order should certainly be not later than time of departure from station (when I went loping over the junkfield with lantern and loot bag racing to catch my guilt late in the gray candy gloom) and ah but all of it sweet. The little curve at Del Monte, the train orders, then the train goes on to mile post 49.1 to the Western Pacific RR crossing, where you always see the track goes directly vertically across this alien track so there is a definite hump in the rail bed, but chickaluck, as we go over, sometimes at dawn returning from Watsonville I'd be dozing in the engine and wondering just about where we were not knowing generally we were in the vicinity of San Jose or Lick and I'd hear the brock a brock and say to myself "The Western Pacific crossing!" and remember how one time a brakee said to me, "Cant sleep nights in this here new house I got here out on Santa Clara avenue for the clatter and racket of that damn engine out there in the midnight" "Why I thought you loved the railroad" "Well to tell you the fact of the matter, is the Western Pacific happens to have a rail running out there" and with such, as tho it was inconceivable that there could be other railroads than the Southern Pacific.—— On we go across the crossing and there we go along the stream, the Oconee of old Jose the little blank blank Guadaloupe river dry and with Indians standing on the banks, that is Mexican children watching the train, and great fields of prickly pear cactus and all green and sweet in the gray afternoon and gonna be golden brown and rich when the sun at five flames flares to throw the California wine over the rearwestern licks into the pacific brine.—— On we go to Lick, always I take my looks at favorite landmarks, some school where boys are practising football in varsity and sub varsity and freshman and sub freshman squads, four of em, under tutelage of raven priests with piping glad voices in the wind, for it's October of footingball heavening rooting root to you.—— Then at Lick there is on a hill a kind of monastery, you barefly see the dreaming marijuana walls of it as you pass, up there, with a bird wheeling to peace, there a field, cloisters, work, cloisterous prayers and every form known to man of sweet mediating going on as we wrangle and back-giggle by with a bursting engine and long knocking space-taking-up half mile long freight any minute I expect a hotbox in, as I look back anxiously, fit to work.

76

—— The dreams of monastery men up there on the hill at Lick, and I think, "Ah creamy walls of either Rome, civilizations, or the last monasterial mediation with God in the didoudkekeghgj" god knows what I'm thinking, and then and my thoughts rapidly change as 101 rears into sight, and Coyote, and the beginning of the sweet fruit fields and prune orchards and the great strawberry fields and the vast fields where you see far off the humble squatting figures of Mexican brazeros in the great haze working to pluck from the earth that which the America with his vast iron wages no longer thinks feasible as an activity yet eats, yet goes on eating, and the brass backs with arms of iron Mexico in the cactus plateau love, they'll do it for us, the railroad freight train and concomitant racks of beets is not even, the men on it, are not even mindful of how those beets or in what mood, sweat, sweetness, were picked —— and laid to rest out of the earth in the steely cradle.—— I see them their bent humble backs remembering my own cotton-picking days in Selma California and I see far off across the grapevines the hills to the west, then the sea, the great sweet hills and further along you begin to see the familiar hill of Morgan Hill, we pass the fields of Perry and Madrone and where they make wine, and it's all there, all sweet the furrows of brown, with blossoms and one time we took a siding to wait for 98 and I ran out there like the hound of the Baskervilles and got me a few old prunes not longer fitten to eat —— the proprietor seeing me, trainman running guiltily back to engine with a stolen prune, always I was running, always was running, running to throw switches, running in my sleep and running now —— happy.

THE SWEETNESS OF THE FIELDS unspeakable —— the names themselves bloody edible like Lick Coyote Perry Madrone Morgan Hill San Martin Rucker Gilroy o sleepy Gilroy Carnadero Corporal Sargent Chittenden Logan Aromas and Watsonville Junction with the Pajaro River passing thru it and we of the railroad pass over its wooded dry Indian draws at somewhere outside Chittenden where one morning all dew pink I saw a little bird sitting on a piece of stanchion straight up wood in the wild tangle, and it was the Bird of Chittenden, and the meaning of morning.—— Sweet enough the fields outside San Jose like at say Lawrence and Sunnyvale and where they have vast harvest and fields with the bentback sad mexicano laborioring in his primavery.—— But once past San Jose somehow the whole California opens ever further, at sunset at Perry or Madrone it is like a dream, you see the little rickety farmhouse, the fields, the rows of green planted fruit, and beyond the green pale mist of hills and over that the red aureoles of pacific sunfall and in the silence the bark of a duog and that fine California night dew already rising ere maw's done wiped the hamburg juice off the frying pan and later on tonite beautiful little Carmelita O' Jose will be gomezing along the road with her brown breasts inside cashmere sweater bouncing ever so slightly even with maidenform bra and her brown feet in thonged sandals also brown, and her dark eyes with pools in em of you wonder what mad meaning, and her arms like arms of handmaidens in the Plutonian bible —— and ladles for her arms, in the form of trees, with juice, take a peach, take the fulsome orange, bit a hole in in, take the orange throw your head back use all your strength and drink and squeeze out the orange thru the hole, all the juice runs down your lip and on her arms.—— She has dust on her toes, and toe nail polish —— she has a tiny brown waist, a little soft chin, soft neck like swan, little voice, little femininity and doesn't know it —— her little voice is little-

78

tinkled.—— Along comes the tired field hand Jose Camero and he see her in the vast sun red in the fruit field moving queen majesty to the well, the tower, he runs for her, the railroad crashes by he pays no attention standing on the engine student brakeman J. L. Kerouac and old hoghead W. H. Sears 12 years in California since leaving the packed Oklahoma dust farms, his father'd in a broken down okie truck ordered departures from there, for the first nonces they were and tried to be cottonpickers and were mighty good at it but one day somebody told Sears to try railroading which he did and then he was now after several years a young fireman, an engineer —— the beautify of the salvation fields of California making no difference to the stone of his eye as with glove framed throttle hand he guides the black beast down the star rail.—— Switches rush up and melt into the rail, sidings part from it like lips, return like lover arms.—— My mind is on the brown knees of Carmelity, the dark spltot between her thighs where creation hides its majesty and all the boys with eager head do rush suffering and want the whole the hole the works the hair the seekme membrane the lovey sucky ducky workjohn, the equalled you, she never able and down goes the sun and it's dark and they're layin in a grape row, nobody can see, or hear, only the dog hears OOO slowly against the dust of that rallroad earth he presses her little behind down to form a little depression in the earth from the force and weight of his tears slowly lunging her downthru and into the portals of her sweetness, and slowly the blood pounds in his indian head and comes to a rise and she softly pants with parted brownly lips and with little pear teeth showing and sticking out just far and just so gently almost biting, burning in the burn of his own, lips —— he drives and thrives to pound, the grain, the grape nod in unison, the wine is springing from the noggin of the ground, bottles will roll on 3rd Street to the sands of Santa Barbara, he's making it with the wouldyou seek it then would and wouldn't you if you too could —— the sweet flesh intermingling, the flowing blood wine dry husk leaf bepiled earth with the hard iron passages going oer, the engine's saying K RRRR OOO AAAWWOOOO and the crossing it's ye famous Krrot Krroot Krroo ooooaaaawwww Kroot —— 2 short one long, one short, 'sa thing I got to learn as one time the hoghead was busy telling a joke in the fireman's ear and we were coming to a crossing and he yelled at me "Go ahead go ahead" and made a pull sign with his hand and I lookied up and grabbed the string and looked out, big engineer, saw the crossing racing up and girls in sandals and tight ass dresses waiting at the flashby RR crossing boards of Carnadero and I let it to, two short pulls, one long, one short, Krroo Krroo Krrrooooa Krut. —— So now it's purple in the sky, the whole rim America falling spilling over the west mountains into the eternal and orient sea, and there's your sad field and lovers twined and the wine is in the earth already and in Watsonville up ahead at the end of my grimy run among a million others sits a bottle of tokay wine which I am going to buy to put some of that earth back in my belly after all this shudder of ferrous knock klock against my soft flesh and bone exultation —— in other words, when work's done, I'm gonna have a drink of wine, and rest. —— The Gilroy Subdivision this is.

THE FIRST RUN I EVER MADE on the Gilroy Subdivision, that night dark and clean, standing by the engine with my lamp and lootbag waiting for the big men to make up their minds here comes this young kid out of the dark, no railroad man but obviously a bummer but on the bum from college or

good family or if not with cleanteeth smile and no
broken down datebag river Jack from the bottoms of
the world night —— said, "This thing going to L.A.?"
—— "Well it's going about part of the way to there,
about 50 miles to Watsonville then if you stick on it
they might route you down to San Luis Obispo too and
that's about halfway to L.A." —— "Ba what d'I care
about halfway to L.A. I want to go all the way to L.A.
—— what are you a railroad brakebanana?" "Yeah,
I'm a student" —— "What's a student" —— "Well it's a
guy learning and getting, well I aint getting paid" (this
being my student chain gang run all the way down)
—— "Ah well I dont like going up and down the same
rail, if you ask me goin to sea is the real life, now that's
where I'm headed or hitch hike to New York, either
way, I wouldnt want to be a railroad man." —— "What
you talkin about man it's great and you're moving all
the time and you make a lot of money and no body
bothers you out there."—— "Neverthefuckingless you
keep going up and down the same rail dont you for
krissakes?" so I told him what how and where boxcar
to get on, "Krissakes dont hurt yourself always remember when you try to go around proving you're a big
adventurer of the American night and wanta you hop
freights like Joel McCrea heroes of old movies Jesus
you dumb son a bitch hang on angel with your tightest
hand and dont let your feet drag under that iron round-
wheel it'll have less regard for the bone of your leg
than it has for this toothpick in my mouty" "Ah you
shitt you shit you think I'm afraid of a goddamn railroad train I'm going off to join the goddam navy and
be on carriers and there's your iron for you I'll land my
airplane half on iron half on water and crashbang and
jet to the moon too." "Good luck to you guy, dont fall
off hang tight grip wrists dont fuck up and tout and
when you gets to L.A. give my regards to Lana Tur-

ner."—— The train was starting to leave and the kid had disappeared up the long black bed and snakeline redcars —— I jumped up on the engine with the regular head man who was going to show me how the run runs, and the fireman, and hoghead.—— Off we chugged, over the crossing, over to the Del Monte curve and where the head man showed me how you hang on with one hand and lean out and crook your arm and grab the train orders off the string —— then out to Lick, the night, the stars. —— Never will forget, the fireman wore a black leather jacket and a white skidrow San Frisco seaman Embarcadero cap, with visor, in the ink of this night he looked exactly like a revolutionary Bridges Curran Bryson hero of old waterfront smosh flops, I could see him with meaty hand waving a club in forgotten union publications rotting in gutters of backalley bars, I could see him with hands deep in pocket going angrily thru the uneccentric unworkingbums of 3rd Street to his rendezvous with the fate of the fish at the waterfront gold blue pier edge where boys sit of afternoons dreaming under clouds on bits of piers with the slap of skeely love waters at their feet, white masts of ships, orange masts of ships with black hulls and all your orient trade pouring in under the Golden Gate, this guy I tell you was like a sea dog not a railroad firemen yet there he sat with his snow white cap in the grimeblack night and rode that fireman's seat like a jockey, chug and we were really racing, they were opening her up wanted to make good time to get past Gilroy before any orders would fuck them up, so across the onlitt tintight and with our big pot 3500 style engine headlights throwing its feverish big lick tongue over the wurrling and incurling and outflying track we go swinging and roaring and flying down that line like fucking madmen and the fireman doesnt exactly hold on to his white hat but he has hand on fire throttle and keeps close eye on valves and tags and steam bubblers and outside looks on the rail and the wind blows his nose back but ee god he bouncing on that seat exactly like a jocket riding a wild horse, why we had a hoghead that night which was my first night so wild he had the throttle opened fullblack and kept yanking at it with one heel against the iron scum of the floor trying to open her up further and if possible tear the locomotive apart to get more out of her and leave the track and fly up in the night over the prune fields, what a magnificent opening night it was for me to ride a fast run like that with a bunch of speed demons and that magnificent fireman with his unpredestined impossible unprecedentable hat white in the black black railroad.—— And all the time and the conversations they have, and the visions in his hat I saw of the public hair restaurant on Howard, how I saw that Frisco California white and gray of rain fogs and the back alleys of bottles, breens, derbies, mustachios of beer, oysters, flying seals, crossing hills, bleak bay windows, eye diddle for old churches with handouts for seadogs barkling and snurling in avenues of lost opportunity time, ah —— loved it all, and the first night the finest night, the blood, "railroading gets in yr blood" the old hoghead is yelling at me as he bounces up and down in his seat and the wind blows his striped cap visor back and the engine like a huge beast is lurching side to side 70 miles per hour breaking all rulebook rules, zomm, zomm, were crashing through the night and out there Carmelity is coming, Jose is making her electricities mix and interrun with his and the whole earth charged with juices turns up the organo to the flower, the unfoldment, the stars bend to it, the whole world's coming as the big engine booms and balls by with the madmen of the white cap California in there flossing and wow there's just no end to all this wine ——

4. SLOBS OF THE KITCHEN SEA

HAVE YOU SEEN A GREAT FREIGHTER
slide by in the bay on a dreamy afternoon and as
you stretch your eyes along the iron serpentine length
in search of people, seamen, ghosts who must be operating this dreaming vessel so softly parting harbor waters
off its steel-shin bow with snout pointed to the Four
Winds of the World you see nothing, no one, not a
soul?

And there it goes in broad daylight, dismal sad
hulk faintly throbbing, incomprehensibly jingling and
jangling in the engine room, chuffing, gently churning
at the rear the buried giant waterscrew onward working
out to sea, eternity, stars of the mad mate's sexton at
rosy Manzanillan night fall offcoast of the sad surf
world —— to skeels of other fisher's bays, mysteries,
opium nights in the porthole kingdoms, narrow main
drags of the Kurd.—— Suddenly my God you realize
you've been looking at some motionless white specks

on the deck, between decks in the house section, and there they are ... the motley messmen in white jackets, they've been leaning all the time motionless like fixed parts of the ship at the galley alleyway hatch.—— It's after dinner, the rest of the crew's well fed and fast asleep in fitful bunks of nap —— themselves such still watchers of the world as they slide out to Time no watcher of the ship can avoid being fooled and scrutinized long before he sees they're human, they're the only living thing in sight.—— Mohammedan Chicos, hideous little Slavs of the sea peering out from witless messcoats —— Negroes with cook hats to crown the shiny tortured forehead black —— by garbage cans of eternity the Latin fellaheen repose and drowse of lullish noon. —— And O the lost insane gulls yowking, falling around in a gray and restless shroud at the moving poop —— O the wake slowly roiling in the churn of the wild propeller that from the engine room on a shaft is being wound and wound by combustions and pressures and irritable labors of Germanic Chief Engineers and Greek Wipers with sweat bandanas and only the Bridge can point this restless energy to some Port of Reason across vast lonesome incredible seas of madness.—— Who's on the forepeak? Who's on the afterdeck? Who's on the flying bridge, mate?—— not a loving soul.—— Old bateau negotiates our sleepy retired bay and heads for the Narrows the mouths of Neptune Osh thinning smalling as we watch —— past beacon —— past point of land —— bleak, grimy, gray thin veil of drowsiness flups from the stack, sends heat waves to heaven —— flags on shrouds wake up to the first sea wind. We can hardly make out the name of the ship painted mournfully on the bow and on a board along the topdeck bulwark.

Soon the first long waves'll make this ship a swelling sea snake, foam will be pressed unfurling at the solemn mouth.—— Where the messboys we saw lean-

ing on that homey afterdishes rail, in sun? They'll have
gone in by now, closed the shutters on the long jail time
of sail at sea time, iron'll be clamped bong and flat dull
as wood on the drunken hopes of Port, the fevered rav-
ing gladnesses of the Embarcadero night first ten drinks
white hats bobbing in a brown pocked bar all blue Frisco
wild with seamen people trolleys restaurants hills night
is now just the sloping whitehill town behind your
Golden Gate bridge, out we go.——

One o'clock. The S.S. *William Carothers* is sailing
to the Panama Canal and Gulf of Mexico.——

One snowy flag of wash flutters from the poop an
emblem of the gone-in messmen's silence.—— Have you
seen them floating out to sea past your commuter's ferry,
your drawbridge driving-to-work Ford, scullionish,
greasy aproned, depraved, evil, seedy as coffee grounds
in a barrel, unimportant as orange peels on an oily deck,
white as seagull dung —— pale as feathers —— birdy ——
demented raunchy slop boys and Sicilian adventurers
of the mustachio Sea? And wondered about their lives?
Georgie Varewsky when I first saw him that morning in
the Union Hall looked so much the part of the spectral
scullion sailing to his obscurity Singapores that I knew
I had seen him a hundred times before —— somewhere
—— and I knew I was going to see him a hundred times
again.

HE HAD THAT WONDERFULLY DEPRAVED
look not only of the dedicated feverish European
Waiter alcoholic but something ratty and sly —— wild,
he peered at no one, was aloof in the hall like an aristo-
crat of some own interior silence and reason to say nothing, as, you will find, all true drinkers in their drinking
sickness which is the reprieve from excitement will have

86

a thin, loose smile vague at the corners of their mouths and be communicant with something deep inside themselves be it revulsion or shuddering hangoveral joy and wont communicate with others for the nonce (thats the business of the screamingdrinking night), will instead stand alone, suffer, smile, inwardly laugh alone, kings of pain.—— His pants were baggy, his tortured jacket must have been crumpled under his head all night.—— Low at the end of one long arm and finger hung a lowly smoking lost butt lit a few hours before and alternately lit and forgotten and crushed and carried blocks across shuddering gray necessary activity.—— You could see by looking at him that he had spent all his money and had to get another ship.—— He stood, slightly bent forward at the waist, ready for any charmingly humorous and otherwise thing to happen.—— Short, blond, Slavic —— he had serpentine cheekbones pearshaped which in drink of nightbefore'd been greased and fevered and now were pale worm skin —— over this his crafty luminous blue eyes slanted looking.—— His hair was thin, baldish, also tortured as if some great God Hand of Drunken Night had given it a grip and a yank —— skewish, thin, ash color, Baltic.—— He had a fuzz of beard —— shoes scuffledown.—— You'd picture him in an immaculate white jacket hair slicked at the sides in Parisian and Transatlantic saloons but even that could never remove that Slavic secret wickedness in his stealthy looks and's only looking at his own shoe tops.—— Lips full, red, rich, pressed and murmured together and as if to mumble "Senevabitch . . ."

The job call came up, I got the bedroom steward job, Georgie Varewski the furtive shivering guilty sick-looking blond got the messman job smiling his wan aristocratic pale faroff smile.—— The name of the ship was S.S. *William Carothers*. We were all supposed to report at a place called the Army Base at 6 A.M. I went right up to my new shipmate and asked him: "Where *is* this Army Base?"

He looked me over with a sly smile —— "I show you. Meet me in bar on 210 Market Street —— Jamy's —— 10 o'clock tonight —— we go in, sleep on the ship, take the A train across the bridge ——"

"Okay, it's a deal."

"Senevabitch I feel much better now."

"What happened." I thought he was relieved he had just gotten a job he thought he wouldnt get.

"I was seek. All last night I drink every goddam thing I see ——"

"What?"

"Mix it."

"Beer? Whiskey?"

"Beer, whiskey, wine —— goddam green d-r-r-ink ——" We were standing outside on the great steps of the hall high above the blue waters of San Francisco Bay, and they were there, the white ships on the tide, and all my love rose to sing my newfound seaman's life.—— The Sea! Real ships! My sweet ship had come in, no dream but true with tangled rigging and actual shipmates and the job slip secure in my wallet and only the night before I'd been kicking cockroaches in my tiny dark room in Third Street slums.—— I felt like hugging my friend.—— "What's your name? This is great!"

"George —— Georg-ee —— I'm a Polock, they call it me, Crazy Polock. Everybody knows it me. I drrreenk and drreenk and vugup all the time and lose my job, miss my ship —— they give it me one more chance —— I was so seek I couldnt see —— now I feel it a little better ——"

"Have a beer, that'll straighten you out ——"

No! I start all over again, I go cr-razy, two, three beers, *boom!* I'm gone, I take it off, you not see me any more." Forlorn smile, shrug. "Is the way it is. Crazy Polock."

"They gave me B.R.—— they gave you Mess."

"They give it me one more chance then is 'Georgie, boom, go away, drop dead, you fired, you no seaman, funny senevabitch, vugup too mach —— I *know*," he grins.—— "They see my eyes, all shining, they say 'Georgie iss drunk again' —— no —— one more beer I cant, —— I not vugup now till we sail ——"

"Where we goin?"

"Mobile load up —— Far East —— probably Japann, Yokohama —— Sasebo —— Kobe —— I don know —— Probably Korrea —— Probably Saigon —— Indo China —— nobody knows —— I show you how to do your work if you are a new man —— I'm Georgie Varewski Crazy Polock —— I dont give it fuk, ——"

"Okay Pal. We'll meet 10 o'clock tonight.——"

"210 Market —— and dont get drrunk and dont show up!"

"And you too! if you miss I'll go alone."

"Dont worry —— I have it no money not a senevabitch cent.—— No money to eat it ——"

"Dont you need a couple bucks to eat?" I took out my wallet.

He looked at me slyly. "You got it?"

"Two bucks sure."

"Okay."

He went off, hands in pants pockets humbly, defeatedly, but on swift determined feet hustling in a straight line to his goal and as I looked I saw he really was walking extremely fast —— head down, bemused upon the world and all the ports of the world he'd go cut in with rapid steps.——

I turned to breathe the great fresh air of harbors, exulting on my good luck —— I pictured myself with grave face pointed seaward through the final Gate of

Golden America never to return, I saw shrouds of gray sea dripping from my prow ——

I never dwelt on the dark farcical furious real life of this roaring working world, wow.

IN ROARING BLOODSHOT OF MY OWN I showed up at 10 o'clock that night without my gear just my seaman buddy Al Sublette who was celebrating my "last night ashore" with me.—— Varewski was sitting deep in the profound bar drinkless, with two drunken drinking seamen.—— He hadnt touched a drop since I'd seen him and with what forlorn discipline eyeing cups proffered and otherwise and all the explanations. —— The swirl of the world was upon this bar as I came reeling in on a slant, the Van Gogh boards flowing to brown slatwall johns, spittoons, scrapetables of the back —— like eternity saloons of Moody Lowell and with the same.—— It's been so, in bars of Tenth Avenue New York I —— and Georgie too —— the first three beers on an October dusk, the glee of scream of children in the iron streets, the wind, the ships in the band of the river —— the way the sparkle glow spreads in the belly giving strength and turning the world from a place of gnash-serious absorption in the details of struggle and complaint, into a gigantic gut joy capable of swelling like a distended shadow by distance hugened and with the same concomitant loss of density and strength so that in the morning after the 30th beer and 10 whiskies and early morning goof vermouths on rooftops, in topcoats, cellars, places of energy subtracted, not added, the more you drink the more there is false strength, false strength is subtractable.—— Flup, the man's dead in the morning, the brown drear happiness of bars and saloons is the whole world's shuddering void and the nerve-ends being slowly living deathly cut in the center

of the gut, the slow paralysis of fingers, hands —— the
spectre and horror of a man once rosy babe now a shivering ghost in cracking surrealist night of cities, forgotten
faces, money hurled, food hurled, drinks, drinks, drinks,
the thousand chewed talks in dimnesses.—— O the joy
of the whitecap seaman or ex seaman wino howling in
a Third Street alley in San Francisco beneath the cat's
moon and even as the solemn ship the Golden Gate
waters shoves aside, bow-watch lonely whiteshirt able-
bodied seaman Japan-pointed on the forepeak with his
sobering cup of coffee, the pocknosed bum of bottles
is ready to crash against narrow walls, invoke his death
in nerveless degrees, find his feeble tape of love in the
winding stool of lonely gloom saloons —— all illusion.

"You senevabitch you d-r-r-onk," laughed Georgie
seeing me roll in eyes wild money dripping from my
pants —— pounding on the bar —— "Beer! beer!" ——
And still he wouldnt drink —— "I no vugup till I get
it ship —— this time I lose for good the union good get
pissyass at me, it's goombye Georgie boom." —— And
his face full of sweat, his sticky eyes avoiding cold foams
at tops of beerglasses, his fingers still clutching a low
smoking butt all begrimed with nicotine and gnarled
from the work of the world.

"Hey man where is your mother?" I yelled seeing
him so alone littleboyish and forsaken in all the brown
complicated millionmoth stress and screaming strain
of drink, work, sweat ——

"She iss in East Poland with my sister.—— She
will not come to West Germany because she iss religious
and stay hum and is proud —— she go to church —— I
send her nothing —— Wat's the use?"

His amigo wanted a dollar out of me.—— "Who
is this?"

"Come on, give it him dollar, you got ship now,
—— he iss seaman ——" I didnt want to but I did give

him the dollar and as Georgie and I and friend Al left he called me a c-sucker for having been so reluctant. —— So I went back to belt him or at least swim around the sea of his insolence a minute and lead him to apologies but all was a blur and I sensed crashing fists and cracking wood and skulls and police wagons in the brown crazy air.—— It staggered somewhere, Georgie left, it was night —— Al left —— I staggered in the lonely night streets of Frisco dimly realizing I must make the ship at six or miss it.

I WOKE UP AT 5 in the morning in my old railroad room with the torn carpet and shade that was drawn over a few feet of soot roof to the endless tragedy of a Chinese family the boy child of which as I say was in continual torment of tears, his pappy slapping him to silence every night, the mother screaming.—— Now at dawn a gray silence in which the fact exploded, "I've missed my ship" —— I still had an hour to make it.—— Picked up my already packed seabag and rushed out —— tottering bagashoulder, in the gray mist of fateful Frisco to go catch my racy A Train for over-the-bay-bridge ride to the Army Base.—— A taxi from the A Train and I was at the ship's slapping hem, her stack with a "T" for Transfuel on it showed over the gray Navy dumpshed.—— I hurried deeper in.—— It was a Liberty ship black with orange booms and blue and orange stack —— WILLIAM H. CAROTHERS —— not a soul in sight —— I ran up the weaving gangplank with my burden bag, tossed it to the deck, looked around. —— Steaming clatters from the galley straight ahead. —— Instantly I knew there'd be trouble when a little ratty German with red eyes began yipping at me about how late I was, I had my railroad watch to prove I was only 12 minutes late but he was raining red sweats of

hatred —— later we called him Hitler.—— A cook with
cool little mustache stepped in:

"He's only 12 minutes late.—— C'mon let's get
breakfast going and talk about it later." ——

"Goddam guys tink dey can come on late and I
wont say nottin.—— You gonna be pantryman," he said
suddenly smiling to ingratiate this nice idea of his.

Pantry *shit* I was about to say but the cook took
me by the arm: "You were sent out as bedroom steward,
you'll be bedroom steward.—— Just for this morning
do what he says.—— You want him to wash the dishes
this morning?"

"Yeh —— We shorthanded."

And already I could feel the steam of a hot Oakland day pressing down on my hangover brow.—— There
was Georgie Varewski smiling at me —— "I get it out
jacket —— we co workers this morning —— I sha you."
—— He took me down the steel horror alleys to the
linen locker, unbearable heat and sorrow that stretched
ahead of my bones only lately I'd at least in bum's freedom stretched at will anytime in hobo exile hotel.——
I was in the Army now —— I gulped down a quick benny
to face the music —— I saved my job.—— From horror
groanings and sleepy nausea at the sink with allnight's
watch and longshore dishes piled I whammed inside
20 minutes into active keen energetic benevolence asking everyone including the ferret steward questions,
gripping people by the arm, leaning, listening to troubles, being kind, working like a dog, doing extras,
absorbing every word instruction Georgie said from
benzedrine despair to love, work, learn.—— sweating
buckets to the steel ——

Suddenly I saw myself in the foc'sle mirror, slick-
haired, ring eyed, whitejacketed sudden-waiter-slave of
scows where a week before I'd walked erect longwaist
on the Plomteau Local, railroad afternoons in drowsy

gravel spurs giving the pot the come ahead with no lapse in dignity when stooping swift to throw a sweet switch.—— Here I was a goddam scullion and it was writ on my greasy brow, and at less pay too.—— All for China, all for the opium dens of Yokohama.——

BREAKFAST SWAM BY IN A DREAM, I raced through everything benny wild, —— it took 24 hours before I even paused to unpack my bag or look out at the waters and call them Oakland's.——

I was taken to my bedroom steward's quarters by the retiring B.R. who was an old pale skinned man from Richmond Hill Long Island (that is, had taken sun baths belowdecks in the glare of dry linens just laundered and stashed).—— Two bunks in one room but horribly placed next to the upsurging fires from the engine room, for a headrest one had the smokestack, it was so hot.—— I looked around in despair.—— The old man was confidential, poked me: —— "Now if you havent been a B.R. before you might have trouble." —— This meant I must look seriously at his white countenance and nod, peer deeply into it, become buried in the vast cosmos of him, learn all —— B.R. all.—— "If you want I'll show you where everything is but I aint s'posed to cause I'm gettin off —— however." —— He did get off, it took him two days to pack, a full hour alone to pull on horribly diseased sad convalescent socks the color was white over his white little thin ankles —— to tie his shoelaces —— to run his finger through the back of his locker, floors, bulkheads for any speck he might've forgotten to pack —— a little sickly belly protruding from the shapelessness of his stick.—— Was this B.R. Jack Kerouac in 1983?

"Well come on, show me what's what! I gotta get goin ——"

"Take it easy, hold your water —— only the captain's up and he aint been down to breakfast.—— I'll show you —— now look —— that's if you wanta —— now I'm getting off and I don't have to" and he forgot what he was gonna say and returned to his white socks.—— There was something of the hospital in him.—— I rushed to find Georgie.—— The ship was one vast new iron nightmare —— no sweet salt sea.

AND THERE I AM staggering around the tragic darkness of the slavish alleyway with brooms, mops, handles, sticks, rags sticking out of me like a sad porcupine —— my face downcast, worried, intent —— aloft in the aerial world from that sweet previous Skid Row bed of underground comfort.—— I have a huge carton (empty) for the dumpings of officers' ashtrays and wastebaskets —— I have two mops, one for toilet floors, one for decks —— a wet rag and dry rag —— emergency shifts and ideas of my own.—— I go frantically searching for my work —— incomprehensible people are trying to get around me in the alleyways to get the work of the ship done.—— After a few desultory hair drooping lugubrious licks at the Chief Mate's floor he comes in from breakfast, chats affably with me, he's going off to be captain on a ship, feels good.—— I comment on the interesting notes in the discarded notebooks in his wastebasket, concerning stars.—— "Go up in the chartroom," he says, "and you'll find a lot of interesting notebooks in the basket up there." —— Later I do and it's locked. —— The captain appears —— I stare at him befuddled, sweaty, waiting.—— He sees at once the idiot with the pail, his crafty brain begins working at once.——

He was a short distinguished looking grayhaired man with hornrim glasses, good sporty clothes, sea green eyes, quiet unassuming look.—— Beneath this lurked an insane mischievous perverted spirit that even at that first moment began to manifest itself when he said "Yes Jack all you have to do is learn to do your job right and everything will be alright —— now as for instance in cleaning —— now look come in here" —— he insisted I go in deep in his quarters, where he could speak low —— "When you —— now look —— you dont ——" (I began to see his mad way in the stutterings, changings of mind, hiccupings of meaning) —— "you dont use the same mop for deck *and* toilet" he said nastily, in a nasty tone, almost snarling and where a minute ago I'd marveled at the dignity of his calling, the great charts on his workdesk, now I wrinkled my nose to realize this idiotic man was all hung up on mops. —— "There's such things as germs, you know," he said, as if I didn't know although little he knew how little I cared about his germs.—— There we were in the California harbor morning consulting on these matters in his immaculate cabin, that thing was like a Kingdom to my skidrow closet and would it make any difference to him anyway not on your life ——

"Yes I'll do it that way, dont worry —— er —— man —— captain —— sir ——" (no idea yet how to sound natural in new sea militarisms).—— His eyes twinkled, he leaned forward, there was something unwholesome and something, some hole card not shown.—— I covered all the officers' rooms doing desultory work not really knowing how and waiting for when Georgie or somebody would show me.—— No time for naps, hungover in the afternoon I had to do the 3rd Cook's scullion work in the galley sink with huge pots and pans till the man came from the union hall.—— He was a big Armenian with close set eyes, fat, weight about 260: he took bites day in day out at his work —— sweet potatoes, pieces of cheese, fruit, he tasted it all and had big meals in between.

96

His room (and mine) was the first in the port alleyway facing forward.—— Next door was the deck engineer, Ted Joyner, alone; oft and many a night at sea he invited me in there for a snort and always with confidential deepsouth florid faced friendly and —— "Now I'm goan tell you the truth, *I* dont really like so-and-so and that's the way I feel, but I'm goan tell you the truth, now, lissen, this is no shit and I'm gonna tell you the truth, it's just a matter of —— well I really dont like it and I'm goan tell you the truth, ah dont mince words —— now do I Jack?" —— nevertheless the prime gentleman of the ship, he was from deep in Florida and weighed also 250 question being who ate most he or Gavril my big 3rd cook roommate, I would say Ted did.

Now I'm going to tell you the truth.

NEXT DOOR were the two Greek wipers, George one, the other never spoke and hardly told his name. —— George from Greece, this being in fact a Greek owned Liberty operating under the American flag which many a time thereafter fluttered over my sleep in afternoon cots on the poop deck.—— When I looked at George I thought of the brown leaves of the Mediterranean, old tawny ports, ouzos and figs of the Isle of Crete or Cyprus, he was that color and had a little mustache and olive green eyes and a sunny disposition.—— Amazing how he took all the kidding from the rest of the crew concerning that Greek predilection to love it up the rear —— "Yey, yey!" he'd laugh scatteringly —— "Up de ass, yey yey." —— His non-committal roommate was a young man before our very eyes in the process of growing old —— still youthful of face and with little lover mustache and still youthful of figure in arms and legs he was growing a pot that looked all out of proportion and seemed bigger every time I watched him after supper.—— Some lost love affair had just made him give up attempts to look young and lover-like I presumed.——

The mess hall was next to their foc'sle —— then Georgie's room, the pantryman's and saloon messman who didnt arrive till the second day —— then at the forward end facing the bow, the Chief Cook and the 2nd Cook and Baker. Chief Cook was Chauncey Preston a Negro also from Florida but way down in the Keys and in fact he had a West Indian look besides regular American Southern Negro of hot fields especially when in there sweating at the range or hammering at beef sections with a cleaver, an excellent cook and sweet person, said to me as I passed with dishes "What you got there love?" and hard and wiry as a boxer, his black figure perfect, you wondered he never got fat on those amazing yams and yam sauces and pigs knuckle stews and Southern Fried Chicken he made. —— But the first wonderful meal he made you heard the deep quiet menacing voice of the blond curlylocks Swedish bosun: "If we dont want our food salted on this ship, we dont want it salted" and Prez answered from the galley in just as deep and quiet a menacing voice "If you dont like it dont eat it." You could see it coming, the trip . . .

The 2nd Cook and Baker was a hipster, a union man, that is a unionist —— a jazz devotee —— a sharp dresser —— a soft, mustached, elegant, pale gold colored cook of the blue seas who said to me "Man, pay no attention to the beefs and the performances on this or any other ship you might hang up on in the future, just do your work the best way you know, and" (wink) "you'll make it —— dad, I'm hep, you understand, right?"

"You got it."

"So just be cool and we'll all be one happy family,

you'll see. What I mean, man, it's people —— that's all —— it's people.—— Chief Cook Prez, is people —— real people —— the captain, the Chief Steward, okay, no.—— We know that —— we stand together ——"

"I'm hip ——"

He was over 6 feet, wore snazzy white and blue canvas shoes, a fantastic rich Japanese silk sports shirt bought coolly in Sasebo —— Beside his bunk a great longdistance Shortwave Zenith portable radio to pick up the bops and shmops of the world from here to hottest Madras —— but let nobody play it unless he was there ——

My big room mate Gavril the 3rd Cook was also hip, also unionist, but a lonely big fat furtive unloving and unloved slob of the sea —— "Man, I have every record Frank Sinatra ever made including *I Cant Get Started* made in New Jersey in 1938" ——

"Dont tell me things are going to look up?" I thought. And there was Georgie, wonderful Georgie and the promise of a thousand drunken nights in the mysterious odorous real ocean-girdled Orient World. —— I was ready.——

After washing galley pots and pans all afternoon, a chore I'd tasted before in 1942 in the gray cold seas of Greenland and now found less demeaning, more like one's proper dive in hell and guilt-earned labor of the steams, punishment in hot water and scald for all the bluesky puffs I'd leaned on lately —— (and a nap at four just before supper dishes) —— I took off for my first night ashore in the company of Georgie and Gavril. We put on clean shirts, combed, went down the gang-plank in the cool of evening: this is sea men.

BUT OH SO TYPICAL OF SEAMEN, that they never do anything —— just go ashore with money in their pockets and amble around dully and even with a kind of uninterested sorrow, visitors from another world, a floating prison, in civilian clothes most uninteresting looking anyway.—— We walked across the Navy's vast supply dumps —— huge graypainted warehouses, sprinklers watering lost lawns that no one wanted or ever used and which ran between tracks of the Navy Yard railroad.—— Immense distances at dusk with no one in sight in the redness.—— Sad groups of sailors swimming their way out of the Giant Macrocosmos to find a Microcosmic bug and go to pleasures of downtown Oakland which are really nil, just streets, bars, jukeboxes with Hawaiian hula girls painted on —— barbershops, desultory liquor stores, the characters of life hanging around.—— I knew the only place to get kicks, to get women, way in the Mexican or Negro streets which were on the outskirts but I followed Georgie and "Heavy" as we later called the 3rd Cook to a bar in Oakland downtown where we just sat in the brown gloom, Georgie not drinking, Heavy fidgeting.—— I drank wine, I didnt know where to go, what do.——

I found a few good Gerry Mulligan records on the box and played them.

BUT THE NEXT DAY we sailed out the Golden Gate in a gray foggy suppertime dusk, before you knew it we had turned the headlands of San Francisco and lost them beneath the gray waves.——

The trip down the West Coast of America and Mexico, again, only this time at sea within full sight of the vague brown coastline where sometimes on clear days I could definitely see the arroyos and canyons of the Southern Pacific rail where it lined along the surf —— like looking at an old dream.

Some nights I slept on deck in a cot and Georgie Varewski said "You senevabitch one morning I wake up you wont be here —— goddam Pacific, you teenk goddam Pacific is quiet ocean? big tidal wave come some night when you dreaming of girls and pof, no more you —— you be washed away."

Holy sunrises and holy sunsets in the Pacific with everybody on board quietly working or reading in their bunks, the booze all gone.—— Calm days, which I'd open at dawn with a grapefruit cut in halves at the rail of the ship, and below me there they were, the smiling porpoise leaping and curlicueing in the wet gray air, sometimes in the powerful driving rains that made sea and rain the same. I wrote a haiku about it:

> *Useless, useless!*
> *—— Heavy rain driving*
> *Into the sea!*

Calm days that I went and fouled up, because I foolishly traded my bedroom job for the dishwasher job, which is the best job on the ship because of sudsy privacy, but then I foolishly transferred to the officers' waiter (saloon messman) and that was the worst shot on the ship. "Why dont you smile nice and say good morning?" said the captain as I laid down his eggs before him.

"I'm not the smiling type."

"Is that the way to present breakfast to an officer? Lay it down gently with both hands."

"Okay."

Meanwhile the Chief Engineer is yelling: "Where's the goddam pineapple juice, I dont want no goddam orange juice!" and I have to run below to the bottom stores so when I get back the Chief Mate is burning because his breakfast's late. The Chief Mate has a full mustache and thinks he's a hero in a Hemingway novel who has to be served punctiliously.

And when we sail through the Panama Canal I

cant keep my eyes off the exotic green trees and leaves,
palms, huts, guys in straw hats, the deep brown warm
tropical mud out there along the banks of the canal
(with South America just over the swamp in Colombia)
but the officers are yelling: "Come on, goddamit, didnt
you ever see the Panama Canal before, where the hell
is lunch?"

We sailed up the Caribbean (blue sparkler) to Mobile Bay and into Mobile where I went ashore, got drunk
with the boys and later went to a hotel room with the
pretty young Rose of Dauphine Street and missed a
morning's work.—— When Rosy and I were walking
hand in hand down Main Street at 10 A.M. (a terrible
sight both of us without underwear or socks, just my
pants, her dress, T-shirts, shoes, walking along drunk,
and she's a cutie too) it was the captain, lurking around
with his tourist camera, who saw it all.—— Back on the
ship they give me hell and I say I'm going to quit in
New Orleans.

So the ship sails from Mobile Alabama westward
to the mouths of the Mississippi in a lightning storm at
midnight which lights up the salt marshes and vast-
nesses of that great hole where all America pours out
her heart, her mud and hopes in one grand falling slam
of water into the doom of the Gulf, the rebirth of the
Void, into the Night.—— There I am drunk on the cot
on deck looking at it all with hungover eyes.

And the ship goes chugging right up the Mississippi River right back into the heart of the American
land where I'd just been hitch hiking, damnit, there
wasnt about to be no Exotic Sasebo for me. Georgie
Varewski looked at me and grinned:—— "Senevabitch
Jackcrack, vugup huh?" The ships goes and docks at
some calm green shore like the shores of Tom Sawyer,
somewhere upriver from La Place, to load on barrels
of oil for Japan.

I collect my pay of about $300, wad it up together with my $300 left from the railroad, heave the dufflebag on back again, and there I go again.

I look into the mess hall where all the boys are sitting around and not one of them is looking at me. —— I feel eerie —— I say "Well when'd they say you're sailing?"

They looked at me blankly, with eyes that didnt see me, as though I was a ghost.—— When Georgie looked at me it was also there in his eyes, a thing that said: "Now that you are no longer a member of the crew, on this ghostly vehicle, you are dead to us." "We cant possibly get any more out of you," I could have added, remembering all the times they insisted on my company for dull smoky bull sessions in bunks with great fat bellies spilling out like blob in the horrible tropical heat, not even one porthole open.—— Or the greasy confidences about malefactions that had no charm.

Prez the Negro chief cook had been fired and was going into town with me and say goodbye on the sidewalks of old New Orleans.—— It was an anti-Negro management —— the captain was worse than anyone else.——

Prez said "I'd sure like to go to New York with ya and go down to Birdland but I gotta get a ship."

We walked off the gangplank in the silence of the afternoon.

The second cook's car en route to New Orleans zoomed by us on the highway.

5. NEW YORK SCENES

AT THIS TIME MY MOTHER was living alone in a little apartment in Jamaica Long Island, working in the shoe factory, waiting for me to come home so I could keep her company and escort her to Radio City once a month. She had a tiny bedroom waiting for me, clean linen in the dresser, clean sheets in the bed. It was a relief after all the sleepingbags and bunks and railroad earth. It was another of the many opportunities she's given me all her life to just stay home and write.

I always give her all my leftover pay. I settled down to long sweet sleeps, day-long meditations in the house, writing, and long walks around beloved old Manhattan a half hour subway ride away. I roamed the streets, the bridges, Times Square, cafeterias, the waterfront, I looked up all my poet beatnik friends and roamed with them, I had love affairs with girls in the Village, I did everything with that great mad joy you get when you return to New York City.

I've heard great singing Negroes call it "The Apple!"

"There now is your insular city of the Manhattoes, belted round by wharves," sang Herman Melville.

"Bound round by flashing tides," sang Thomas Wolfe.

Whole panoramas of New York everywhere, from New Jersey, from skyscrapers.——

EVEN FROM BARS, like a Third Avenue bar —— 4 P.M. the men are all roaring in clink bonk glass brass-foot barrail "where ya goin" excitement —— October's in the air, in the Indian Summer sun of door.—— Two Madison Avenue salesmen who been working all day long come in young, well dressed, justsuits, puffing cigars, glad to have the day done and the drink comin in, side by side march in smiling but there's no room at the roaring (Shit!) crowded bar so they stand two deep from it waiting and smiling and talking.—— Men do love bars and good bars should be loved.—— It's full of businessmen, workmen, Finn MacCools of Time.—— Be-overalled oldgray topers dirty and beerswiggin glad. —— Nameless truck busdrivers with flashlites slung from hips —— old beatfaced beerswallowers sadly upraising purple lips to happy drinking ceilings.—— Bartenders are fast, courteous, interested in their work as well as clientele.—— Like Dublin at 4:30 P.M. when the work is done, but this is great New York Third Avenue, free lunch, smells of Moody street exhaust river lunch in road of grime bysmashing the door, guitarplaying long sideburned heroes smell out there on wood doorsteps of afternoon drowse.—— But it's New York towers rise beyond, voices crash mangle to talk and chew the gossip till Earwicker drops his load —— Ah Jack Fitzgerald Mighty Murphy where are you?.—— Semi bald blue shirt tattered shovellers in broken end dungarees fisting glasses of glistenglass foam top brown afternoon beer.—— The subway rumbles underneath as man in homburg in vest but coatless executive changes from right to left foot on ye brass rail.—— Colored man in hat, dignified, young, paper underarm, says goodbye at bar warm and paternal leaning over men —— elevator operator around the corner.—— And wasnt this where they say Novak the real estator who used to stay up late a-nights linefaced to become right and rich in his little white worm cellule of the night typing up reports and letters wife and kids go mad at home at eleven P.M. —— ambitious, worried, in a little office of the Island, right on the street undignified but open to all business and in infancy any business can be small as ambition's big —— pushing how many daisies now? and never made his million, never had a drink with So Long Gee Gee and I Love You Too in this late afternoon beer room of men excited shifting stools and footbottom rail scuffle heel soles in New York? —— Never called Old Glasses over and offered his rim red nose a drink —— never laughed and let the fly his nose use as a landingmark —— but ulcerated in the middle of the night to be rich and get his family the best.—— So the best American sod's his blanket now, made in upper mills of Hudson Bay Moonface Sassenach and carted down by housepainter in white coveralls (silent) to rim the roam of his once formed flesh, and let worms ram —— Rim! So have another beer, topers —— Bloody mugglers! Lovers!

MY FRIENDS AND I in New York city have our own special way of having fun without having to spend much money and most important of all without having to be importuned by formalistic bores, such as, say, a swell evening at the mayor's ball.—— We dont have to shake hands and we dont have to make appointments and we feel all right.—— We sorta wander around like children.—— We walk into parties and tell everybody what we've been doing and people think we're showing off.—— They say: "Oh look at the beatniks!"

Take, for example, this typical evening you can have: ——

Emerging from the Seventh Avenue subway on 42nd Street, you pass the john, which is the beatest john in New York —— you never can tell if it's open or not, usually there's a big chain in front of it saying it's out of order, or else it's got some white-haired decaying monster slinking outside, a john which all seven million people in New York City have at one time passed and taken strange notice of —— past the new charcoal-fried-hamburger stand, Bible booths, operatic jukeboxes, and a seedy underground used-magazine store next to a peanut-brittle store smelling of subway arcades —— here and there a used copy of that old bard Plotinus sneaked in with the remainders of collections of German high-school textbooks —— where they sell long ratty-looking hotdogs (no, actually they're quite beautiful, particularly if you havent got 15 cents and are looking for someone in Bickford's Cafeteria who can lay some smash on you) (lend you some change).——

Coming up that stairway, people stand there for hours and hours drooling in the rain, with soaking wet umbrellas —— lots of boys in dungarees scared to go into the Army standing halfway up the stairway on the iron steps waiting for God Who knows what, certainly among them some romantic heroes just in from Oklahoma with ambitions to end up yearning in the arms of some unpredictable sexy young blonde in a penthouse on the Empire State Building —— some of them probably stand there dreaming of owning the Empire

State Building by virtue of a magic spell which they've dreamed up by a creek in the backwoods of a ratty old house on the outskirts of Texarkana.—— Ashamed of being seen going into the dirty movie (what's its name?) across the street from the New York *Times* —— The lion and the tiger passing, as Tom Wolfe used to say about certain types passing that corner.——

Leaning against that cigar store with a lot of telephone booths on the corner of 42nd and Seventh where you make beautiful telephone calls looking out into the street and it gets real cozy in there when it's raining outside and you like to prolong the conversation, who do you find? Basketball teams? Basketball coaches? All those guys from the rollerskating rink go there? Cats from the Bronx again, looking for some action, really looking for romance? Strange duos of girls coming out of dirty movies? Did you ever see them? Or bemused drunken businessmen with their hats tipped awry on their graying heads staring catatonically upward at the signs floating by on the Times Building, huge sentences about Khrushchev reeling by, the populations of Asia enumerated in flashing lightbulbs, always five hundred periods after each sentence.—— Suddenly a psychopathically worried policeman appears on the corner and tells everybody to go away.—— This is the center of the greatest city the world has ever known and this is what beatniks do here.—— "Standing on the street corner waiting for no one is Power," sayeth poet Gregory Corso.

Instead of going to night clubs —— if you're in a position to make the nightclub scene (most beatniks rattle empty pockets passing Birdland) —— how strange to stand on the sidewalk and just watch that weird eccentric from Second Avenue looking like Napoleon going by feeling cooky crumbs in his pocket, or a young 15-year-old kid with a bratty face, or suddenly somebody swishing by in a baseball hat (because that's what you see), and finally an old lady dressed in seven hats and a long ratty fur coat in the middle of the July night carrying a huge Russian woolen purse filled with scribbled bits of paper which say "Festival Foundation Inc., 70,000 Germs" and moths flying out of her sleeve —— she rushes up and importunes Shriners. And dufflebag soliders without a war —— harmonica players off freight trains.—— Of course there are the normal New Yorkers, looking ridiculously out of place and as odd as their own neat oddity, carrying pizzas and *Daily Newses* and headed for brown basements or Pennsylvania trains —— W. H. Auden himself may be seen fumbling by in the rain —— Paul Bowles, natty in a Dacron suit, passing through on a trip from Morocco, the ghost of Herman Melville himself followed by Bartleby the Wall Street Scrivener and Pierre the ambiguous hipster of 1848 out on a walk —— to see what's up in the news flashes of the *Times* —— Let's go back to the corner newsstand. —— SPACE BLAST ... POPE WASHES FEET OF POOR ...

Let's go across the street to Grant's, our favored dining place. For 65 cents you get a huge plate of fried clams, a lot of French fried potatoes, a little portion of cole slaw, some tartar sauce, a little cup of red sauce for fish, a slice of lemon, two slices of fresh rye bread, a pat of butter, another ten cents brings a glass of rare birch beer.—— What a ball it is to eat here! Migrations of Spaniards chewing on hotdogs, standing up, leaning against big pots of mustard.—— Ten different counters with different specialties.—— Ten-cent cheese sandwiches, two liquor bars for the Apocalypse, oh yeah and great indifferent bartenders.—— And cops that stand in the back getting free meals —— drunken saxophone players on the nod ——lonely dignified ragpickers from Hudson Street supping soup without a word to anybody, with black fingers, woe.—— Twenty thousand customers a day —— fifty thousand on rainy days —— one hundred thousand on snowy days.—— Operation twenty-four hours a night. Privacy —— supreme under a glary red light full of conversation.—— Toulouse-Lautrec, with his deformity and cane, sketching in the corner.—— You can stay there for five minutes and gobble up your food, or else stay there for hours having insane philosophical conversation with your buddy and wondering about the people.—— "Let's have a hotdog before we go to the movie!" and you get so high in there you never get to the movies because it's better than a show about Doris Day on a holiday in the Caribbean.

"But what are we gonna do tonight? Marty would go to a movie but we're going to connect for some junk. —— Let's go down to the Automat."

"Just a minute, I've got to shine my shoes on top of a fire hydrant."

"You wanta see yourself in the fun mirror?"

"Wanta take four pictures for a quarter? Because we're on the eternal scene. We can look at the picture and remember it when we're wise old white-haired Thoreaus in cabins."

"Ah, the fun mirrors are gone, they used to have fun mirrors here."

"How about the Laff Movie?"

"That's gone too."

"They got the flea circus."

"They still got donzinggerls?"

"The burlesque is gone millions and millions of years ago."

"Shall we go down by the Automat and watch the old ladies eating beans, or the deaf-mutes that stand in front of the window there and you watch 'em and try to figure the invisible language as it flees across the window from face to face and finger to finger . . . ? Why does Times Square feel like a big room?"

Across the street is Bickford's, right in the middle of the block under the Apollo Theater marquee and right next door to a little bookshop that specializes in Havelock Ellis and Rabelais with thousands of sex fiends leafing at the bins.—— Bickford's is the greatest stage on Times Square —— many people have hung around there for years man and boy searching God alone knows for what, maybe some angel of Times Square who would make the whole big room home, the old homestead —— civilization needs it.—— What's Times Square doing there anyway? Might as well enjoy it.—— Greatest city the world has ever seen.—— Have they got a Times Square on Mars? What would the Blob do on Times Square? Or St. Francis?

A girl gets off a bus in the Port Authority Terminal and goes into Bickford's, Chinese girl, red shoes, sits down with coffee, looking for daddy.

There's a whole floating population around Times Square that has always made Bickford's their headquarters day and night. In the old days of the beat generation some poets used to go in there to meet the famous character "Hunkey" who used to come in and out in an oversized black raincoat and a cigarette holder looking for sombody to lay a pawnticket on —— Remington typewriter, portable radio, black raincoat —— to score for some toast, (get some money) so he can go uptown and get in trouble with the cops or any of his boys. Also a lot of stupid gangsters from 8th Avenue used to cut in —— maybe they still do —— the ones from the early days are all in jail or dead. Now the poets just go there and smoke a peace pipe, looking for the ghost of Hunkey or his boys, and dream over the fading cups of tea.

The beatniks make the point that if you went there

every night and stayed there you could start a whole
Dostoevski season on Times Square by yourself and
meet all the midnight newspaper peddlers and their
involvements and families and woes — religious fa-
natics who would take you home and give you long
sermons over the kitchen table about the "new apocalypse" and similar ideas: — "My Baptist minister
back in Winston-Salem told me the reason that God
invented television was that when Christ comes back
to earth again they shall crucify Him right on the streets
of this here Babylon and they gonna have television
cameras pointin' down on that spot and the streets shall
run with blood and every eye shall see."

Still hungry, go out down to the Oriental Cafeteria
— "favored dining spot" also — some night life —
cheap — down in the basement across the street from
the Port Authority monolith bus terminal on 40th Street
and eat big oily lambs' heads with Greek rice for 90¢.
— Oriental zig-zag tunes on the jukebox.

Depends how high you are by now — assuming
you've picked up on one of the corners — say 42nd
Street and 8th Avenue, near the great Whelan's drug
store, another lonely haunt spot where you can meet people — Negro whores, ladies limping in a Benzedrine
psychosis.— Across the street you can see the ruins of
New York already started — the Globe Hotel being
torn down there, an empty tooth hole right on 44th
Street — and the green McGraw-Hill building gaping up in the sky, higher than you'd believe — lonely
all by itself down towards the Hudson River where
freighters wait in the rain for their Montevideo lime-
stone.—

Might as well go on home. It's getting old.—
Or: "Let's make the Village or go to the Lower East
Side and play Symphony Sid on the radio — or play
our Indian records — and eat big dead Puerto Rican

steaks —— or lung stew —— see if Bruno has slashed any more car roofs in Brooklyn —— though Bruno's gentled now, maybe he's written a new poem."

Or look at Television. Night life —— Oscar Levant talking about his melancholia on the Jack Paar show.

The Five Spot on 5th Street and Bowery sometimes features Thelonious Monk on the piano and you go on there. If you know the proprietor you sit down at the table free with a beer, but if you dont know him you can sneak in and stand by the ventilator and listen. Always crowded weekends. Monk cogitates with deadly abstraction, clonk, and makes a statement, huge foot beating delicately on the floor, head turned to one side listening, entering the piano.

Lester Young played there just before he died and used to sit in the back kitchen between sets. My buddy poet Allen Ginsberg went back and got on his knees and asked him what he would do if an atom bomb fell on New York. Lester said he would break the window in Tiffany's and get some jewels anyway. He also said, "What you doin' on your knees?" not realizing he is a great hero of the beat generation and now enshrined. The Five Spot is darkly lit, has weird waiters, good music always, sometimes John "Train" Coltrane showers his rough notes from his big tenor horn all over the place. On weekends parties of well-dressed uptowners jam-pack the place talking continuously —— nobody minds.

O for a couple of hours, though, in the Egyptian Gardens in the lower West Side Chelsea district of Greek restaurants.—— Glasses of ouzo, Greek liqueur, and beautiful girls dancing the belly dance in spangles and beaded bras, the incomparable Zara on the floor and weaving like mystery to the flutes and tingtang beats of Greece —— when she's not dancing she sits in the orchestra with the men plapping a drum against her belly, dreams in her eyes.—— Huge crowds of what appear to be Suburbia couples sit at the tables clapping to the swaying Oriental idea.—— If you're late you have to stand along the wall.

Wanta dance? The Garden Bar on Third Avenue where you can do fantastic sprawling dances in the dim back room to a jukebox, cheap, the waiter doesnt care.

Wanta just talk? The Cedar Bar on University Place where all the painters hang out and a 16-year-old kid who was there one afternoon squirting red wine out of a Spanish wine skin into his friends' mouths and kept missing. . . .

The night clubs of Greenwich Village known as the Half Note, the Village Vanguard, the Café Bohemia, the Village Gate also feature jazz (Lee Konitz, J. J. Johnson, Miles Davis), but you've got to have mucho money and it's not so much that you've got to have mucho money but the sad commercial atmosphere is killing jazz and jazz *is* killing itself there, because jazz belongs to open joyful ten-cent beer joints, as in the beginning.

There's a big party at some painter's loft, wild loud flamenco on the phonograph, the girls suddenly become all hips and heels and people try to dance between their flying hair.—— Men go mad and start tackling people, flying wedges hurtle across the room, men grab men around the knees and lift them nine feet from the floor and lose their balance and nobody gets hurt, blonk.—— Girls are balanced hands on men's knees, their skirts falling and revealing frills on their thighs.—— Finally everybody dresses to go home and the host says dazedly.—— "You all look so *respectable*."

Or somebody just had an opening, or there's a poetry reading at the Living Theater, or at the Gaslight Café, or at the Seven Arts Coffee Gallery, up around Times Square (9th Avenue and 43rd Street, amazing spot) (begins at midnight Fridays), where afterward everybody rushes out to the old wild bar.—— Or else a huge party at Leroi Jones's —— he's got a new issue of Yugen Magazine which he printed himself on a little cranky machine and everybody's poems are in it, from San Francisco to Gloucester Mass., and costs only 50 cents.—— Historic publisher, secret hipster of the trade. —— Leroi's getting sick of parties, everyone's always taking off his shirt and dancing, three sentimental girls are crooning over poet Raymond Bremser, my buddy Gregory Corso is arguing with a New York *Post* reporter saying, "But you dont understand Kangaroonian weep! Forsake thy trade! Flee to the Enchenedian Islands!"

Let's get out of here, it's too literary.—— Let's go get drunk on the Bowery or eat those long noodles and tea in glasses at Hong Pat's in Chinatown.—— What are we always eating for? Let's walk over the Brooklyn Bridge and build up another appetite.—— How about some okra on Sands Street?

Shades of Hart Crane!

"LET'S GO SEE if we can find Don Joseph!"

"Who's Don Joseph?"

Don Joseph is a terrific cornet player who wanders around the Village with his little mustache and his arms hangin at the sides with the cornet, which creaks when he plays softly, nay whispers, the greatest sweetest cornet since Bix and more.—— He stands at the jukebox in the bar and plays with the music for a beer.—— He looks like a handsome movie actor.—— He's the great super glamorous secret Bobby Hackett of the jazz world.

What about that guy Tony Fruscella who sits cross-legged on the rug and plays Bach on his trumpet, by ear, and later on at night there he is blowing with the guys at a session, modern jazz ——

Or George Jones the secret Bowery shroud who plays great tenor in parks at dawn with Charley Mariano, for kicks, because they love jazz, and that time on the waterfront at dawn they played a whole session as the guy beat on the dock with a stick for the beat.

Talkin of Bowery shrouds, what about Charley Mills walkin down the street with bums drinkin his bottle of wine singing in twelve tone scale.

"Let's go see the strange great secret painters of America and discuss their paintings and their visions with them —— Iris Brodie with her delicate fawn Byzantine filigree of Virgins ——"

"Or Miles Forst and his black bull in the orange cave."

"Or Franz Klein and his spiderwebs."

"His bloody spiderwebs!"

"Or Willem de Kooning and his White."

"Or Robert De Niro."

"Or Dody Muller and her Annunciations in seven feet tall flowers."

"Or Al Leslie and his giant feet canvases."

"Al Leslie's giant is sleeping in the Paramount building."

There's another great painter, his name is Bill Heine, he's a really secret subterranean painter who sits with all those weird new cats in the East Tenth street coffeeshops that dont look coffeeshops at all but like sorta Henry Street basement secondhand clothes stores except you see an African sculpture or maybe a Mary Frank sculpture over the door and inside they play Frescobaldi on the hi fi.

AH, LET'S GO BACK TO THE VILLAGE and stand on the corner of Eighth Street and Sixth Avenue and watch the intellectuals go by.—— AP reporters lurching home to their basement apartments on Washington Square, lady editorialists with huge German police dogs breaking their chains, lonely dikes melting by, unknown experts on Sherlock Holmes with blue fingernails going up to their rooms to take scopolamine, a muscle-bound young man in a cheap gray German suit explaining something weird to his fat girl friend, great editors leaning politely at the newsstand buying the early edition of the *Times*, great fat furniture movers out of 1910 Charlie Chaplin films coming home with great bags full of chop suey (feeding everybody), Picasso's melancholy harlequin now owner of a print and frame shop musing on his wife and newborn child lifting up his finger for a taxi, rolypoly recording engineers rush in fur hats, girl artists down from Columbia with D. H. Lawrence problems picking up 50-year-old men, old men in the Kettle of Fish, and the melancholy spectre of New York Women's prison that looms high and is folded in silence as the night itself —— at sunset their windows look like oranges —— poet e. e. cummings buying a package of cough drops in the shade of that monstrosity.—— If it's raining you can stand under the awning in front of Howard Johnson's and watch the street from the other side.

Beatnik Angel Peter Orlovsky in the supermarket five doors away buying Uneeda Biscuits (late Friday night), ice cream, caviar, bacon, pretzels, sodapop, *TV Guide*, Vaseline, three toothbrushes, chocolate milk (dreaming of roast suckling pig), buying whole Idaho potatoes, raisin bread, wormy cabbage by mistake, and fresh-felt tomatoes and collecting purple stamps.—— Then he goes home broke and dumps it all on the table, takes out a big book of Mayakovsky poems, turns on the 1949 television set to the horror movie, and goes to sleep.

And this is the beat night life of New York.

6. ALONE ON A MOUNTAINTOP

AFTER ALL THIS KIND OF FANFARE, and even more, I came to a point where I needed solitude and just stop the machine of "thinking" and "enjoying" what they call "living," I just wanted to lie in the grass and look at the clouds —

They say, too, in ancient scripture: — "Wisdom can only be obtained from the viewpoint of solitude."

And anyway I was sick and tired of all the ships and railroads and Times Squares of all time —

I applied with the U.S. Agriculture Department for a job as a fire lookout in the Mount Baker National Forest in the High Cascades of the Great Northwest.

Just to look at these words made me shiver to think of cool pine trees by a morning lake.

I beat my way out to Seattle three thousand miles from the heat and dust of eastern cities in June.

ANYBODY WHO'S BEEN TO SEATTLE and missed Alaskan Way, the old water front, has missed the point —— here the totem-pole stores, the waters of Puget Sound washing under old piers, the dark gloomy look of ancient warehouses and pier sheds, and the most antique locomotives in America switching boxcars up and down the water front, give a hint, under the pure cloud-mopped sparkling skies of the Northwest, of great country to come. Driving north from Seattle on Highway 99 is an exciting experience because suddenly you see the Cascade Mountains rising on the northeast horizon, truly *Komo Kulshan* under their uncountable snows.—— The great peaks covered with trackless white, worlds of huge rock twisted and heaped and sometimes almost spiraled into fanstastic unbelievable shapes.

All this is seen far above the dreaming fields of the Stilaquamish and Skagit valleys, agricultural flats of peaceful green, the soil so rich and dark it is proudly referred to by inhabitants as second only to the Nile in fertility. At Milltown Washington your car rolls over the bridge across the Skagit River.—— To the left —— seaward, westward —— the Skagit flows into Skagit Bay and the Pacific Ocean.—— At Burlington you turn right and head for the heart of the mountains along a rural valley road through sleepy little towns and one bustling agricultural market center known as Sedro-Woolley with hundreds of cars parked aslant on a typical country-town Main Street of hardware stores, grain-and-feed stores and five-and-tens.—— On deeper into the deepening valley, cliffs rich with timber appearing by the side of the road, the narrowing river rushing more swiftly now, a pure translucent green like the green of the ocean on a cloudy day but a saltless rush of melted snow from the High Cascades —— almost good enough to drink north of Marblemount.—— The road curves more and more till you reach Concrete, the last town in Skagit

Valley with a bank and a five-and-ten —— after that the
mountains rising secretly behind foothills are so close
that now you don't see them but begin to feel them
more and more.

At Marblemount the river is a swift torrent, the
work of the quiet mountains.—— Fallen logs beside the
water provide good seats to enjoy a river wonderland,
leaves jiggling in the good clean northwest wind seem
to rejoice, the topmost trees on nearby timbered peaks
swept and dimmed by low-flying clouds seem contented.
—— The clouds assume the faces of hermits or of nuns,
or sometimes look like sad dog acts hurrying off into the
wings over the horizon.—— Snags struggle and gurgle
in the heaving bulk of the river.—— Logs rush by at
twenty miles an hour. The air smells of pine and saw-
dust and bark and mud and twigs —— birds flash over
the water looking for secret fish.

As you drive north across the bridge at Marblemount and on to Newhalem the road narrows and twists
until finally the Skagit is seen pouring over rocks, frothing, and small creeks come tumbling from steep hillsides
and pile right in.—— The mountains rise on all sides,
only their shoulders and ribs visible, their heads out of
sight and now snowcapped.

At Newhalem extensive road construction raises a
cloud of dust over shacks and cats and rigs, the dam
there is the first in a series that create the Skagit water-
shed which provides all the power for Seattle.

The road ends at Diablo, a peaceful company settle-
ment of neat cottages and green lawns surrounded by
close packed peaks named Pyramid and Colonial and
Davis.—— Here a huge lift takes you one thousand feet
up to the level of Diablo Lake and Diablo Dam.——
Over the dam pours a jet roar of water through which a
stray log could go shooting out like a toothpick
in a one-thousand-foot arc.—— Here for the first time

you're high enough really to begin to see the Cascades. Dazzles of light to the north show where Ross Lake sweeps back all the way to Canada, opening a view of the Mt. Baker National Forest as spectacular as any vista in the Colorado Rockies.

The Seattle City Light and Power boat leaves on regular schedule from a little pier near Diablo Dam and heads north between steep timbered rocky cliffs toward Ross Dam, about half an hour's ride. The passengers are power employees, hunters and fishermen and forestry workers. Below Ross Dam the footwork begins —— you must climb a rocky trail one thousand feet to the level of the dam. Here the vast lake opens out, disclosing small resort floats offering rooms and boats for vacationists, and just beyond, the floats of the U.S. Forestry Service. From this point on, if you're lucky enough to be a rich man or a forest-fire lookout, you can get packed into the North Cascade Primitive Area by horse and mule and spend a summer of complete solitude.

I WAS A FIRE LOOKOUT and after two nights of trying to sleep in the boom and slap of the Forest Service floats, they came for me one rainy morning —— a powerful tugboat lashed to a large corral float bearing four mules and three horses, my own groceries, feed, batteries and equipment.—— The muleskinner's name was Andy and he wore the same old floppy cowboy hat he'd worn in Wyoming twenty years ago. "Well, boy, now we're gonna put you away where we cant reach ya —— you better get ready."

"It's just what I want, Andy, be alone for three solid months nobody to bother me."

"It's what you're sayin' now but you'll change your tune after a week."

I didnt believe him.—— I was looking forward to

an experience men seldom earn in this modern world: complete and comfortable solitude in the wilderness, day and night, sixty-three days and nights to be exact. We had no idea how much snow had fallen on my mountain during the winter and Andy said: "If there didnt it means you gotta hike two miles down that hard trail every day or every other day with two buckets, boy. I aint envyin' you —— I been back there. And one day it's gonna be hot and you're about ready to broil, and bugs you cant even count 'em, and next day a li'l' ole summer blizzard come hit you around the corner of Hozomeen which sits right there near Canada in your back yard and you wont be able to stick logs fast enough in that potbelly stove of yours."
—— But I had a full rucksack loaded with turtleneck sweaters and warm shirts and pants and long wool socks bought on the Seattle water front, and gloves and an earmuff cap, and lots of instant soup and coffee in my grub list.

"Shoulda brought yourself a quart of brandy, boy," says Andy shaking his head as the tug pushed our corral float up Ross Lake through the log gate and around to the left dead north underneath the immense rain shroud of Sourdough Mountain and Ruby Mountain.

"Where's Desolation Peak?" I asked, meaning my own mountain (*A mountain to be kept forever*, I'd dreamed all that spring) (O lonesome traveler!)

"You aint gonna see it today till we're practically on top it and by that time you'll be so soakin' wet you wont care."

Assistant Ranger Marty Gohlke of Marblemount Ranger Station was with us too, also giving me tips and instructions. Nobody seemed to envy Desolation Peak except me. After two hours pushing through the storming waves of the long rainy lake with dreary misty timber rising steeply on both sides and the mules and horses chomping on their feedbags patient in the downpour, we arrived at the foot of Desolation Trail and the tugman (who'd been providing us with good hot coffee in the pilot cabin) eased her over and settled the float against a steep muddy slope full of bushes and fallen trees.—— The muleskinner whacked the first mule and she lurched ahead with her double-sided pack of batteries and canned goods, hit the mud with forehoofs, scrambled, slipped, almost fell back in the lake and finally gave one mighty heave and went skittering out of sight in the fog to wait on the trail for the other mules and her master.—— We all got off, cut the barge loose, waved to the tug man, mounted our horses and started up a sad and dripping party in heavy rain.

At first the trail, always steeply rising, was so dense with shrubbery we kept getting shower after shower from overhead and against our out-saddled knees.—— The trail was deep with round rocks that kept causing the animals to slip.—— At one point a great fallen tree made it impossible to go on until Old Andy and Marty went ahead with axes and cleared a short cut around the tree, sweating and cursing and hacking as I watched the animals.—— By-and-by they were ready but the mules were afraid of the rough steepness of the short cut and had to be prodded through with sticks.—— Soon the trail reached alpine meadows powdered with blue lupine everywhere in the drenching mists, and with little red poppies, tiny-budded flowers as delicate as designs on a small Japanese teacup.—— Now the trail zigzagged widely back and forth up the high meadow. —— Soon we saw the vast foggy heap of a rock-cliff face above and Andy yelled "Soon's we get up high as that we're almost there but that's another two thousand feet though you think you could reach up and touch it!"

I unfolded my nylon poncho and draped it over my head, and, drying a little, or, rather, ceasing to drip,

I walked alongside the horse to warm my blood and began to feel better. But the other boys just rode along with their heads bowed in the rain. As for altitude all I could tell was from some occasional frightening spots on the trail where we could look down on distant tree-tops.

The alpine meadow reached to timber line and suddenly a great wind blew shafts of sleet on us.—— "Gettin' near the top now!" yelled Andy —— and suddenly there was snow on the trail, the horses were chumping through a foot of slush and mud, and to the left and right everything was blinding white in the gray fog.—— "About five and a half thousand feet right now" said Andy rolling a cigarette as he rode in the rain.——

We went down, then up another spell, down again, a slow gradual climb, and then Andy yelled "There she is!" and up ahead in the mountaintop gloom I saw a little shadowy peaked shack standing alone on the top of the world and gulped with fear:

"This my home all summer? And *this* is summer?"

The inside of the shack was even more miserable, damp and dirty, leftover groceries and magazines torn to shreds by rats and mice, the floor muddy, the windows impenetrable.—— But hardy Old Andy who'd been through this kind of thing all his life got a roaring fire crackling in the potbelly stove and had me lay out a pot of water with almost half a can of coffee in it saying "Coffee aint no good 'less it's *strong!*" and pretty soon the coffee was boiling a nice brown aromatic foam and we got our cups out and drank deep.——

Meanwhile I'd gone out on the roof with Marty and removed the bucket from the chimney and put up the weather pole with the anemometer and done a few other chores —— when we came back in Andy was frying Spam and eggs in a huge pan and it was almost like a party.—— Outside, the patient animals chomped on their supper bags and were glad to rest by the old corral fence built of logs by some Desolation lookout of the Thirties.

Darkness came, incomprehensible.

In the gray morning after they'd slept in sleeping bags on the floor and I on the only bunk in my mummy bag, Andy and Marty left, laughing, saying, "Well, whatayou think now hey? We been here twelve hours and you still aint been able to see more than twelve feet!"

"By gosh that's right, what am I going to do for watching fires?"

"Dont worry boy, these clouds'll roll away and you'll be able to see a hunnerd miles in every direction."

I didn't believe it and I felt miserable and spent the day trying to clean up the shack or pacing twenty careful feet each way in my "yard" (the ends of which appeared to be sheer drops into silent gorges), and I went to bed early.—— About bedtime I saw my first star, briefly, then giant phantom clouds billowed all around me and the star was gone.—— But in that instant I thought I'd seen a mile-down maw of grayblack lake where Andy and Marty were back in the Forest Service boat which had met them at noon.

In the middle of the night I woke up suddenly and my hair was standing on end —— I saw a huge black shadow in my window.—— Then I saw that it had a star above it, and realized that this was Mt. Hozomeen (8080 feet) looking in my window from miles away near Canada.—— I got up from the forlorn bunk with the mice scattering underneath and went outside and gasped to see black mountain shapes gianting all around, and not only that but the billowing curtains of the northern lights shifting behind the clouds.—— It was a little too much for a city boy —— the fear that the Abominable Snowman might be breathing behind me in the dark sent me back to bed where I buried my head inside my sleeping bag.——

But in the morning —— Sunday, July sixth —— I was amazed and overjoyed to see a clear blue sunny sky and down below, like a radiant pure snow sea, the clouds making a marshmallow cover for all the world and all the lake while I abided in warm sunshine among hundreds of miles of snow-white peaks.—— I brewed coffee and sang and drank a cup on my drowsy warm doorstep.

At noon the clouds vanished and the lake appeared below, beautiful beyond belief, a perfect blue pool twenty five miles long and more, and the creeks like toy creeks and the timber green and fresh everywhere below and even the joyous little unfolding liquid tracks of vacationists' fishingboats on the lake and in the lagoons.—— A perfect afternoon of sun, and behind the shack I discovered a snowfield big enough to provide me with buckets of cold water till late September.

My job was to watch for fires. One night a terrific lightning storm made a dry run across the Mt. Baker National Forest without any rainfall.—— When I saw that ominous black cloud flashing wrathfully toward me I shut off the radio and laid the aerial on the ground and waited for the worst.—— Hiss! hiss! said the wind, bringing dust and lightning nearer.—— Tick! said the lightning rod, receiving a strand of electricity from a strike on nearby Skagit Peak.—— Hiss! tick! and in my bed I felt the earth move.—— Fifteen miles to the south, just east of Ruby Peak and somewhere near Panther Creek, a large fire raged, a huge orange spot.—— At ten o'clock lightning hit it again and it flared up dangerously.——

I was supposed to note the general area of lightning strikes.—— By midnight I'd been staring so intently out the dark window I got hallucinations of fires everywhere, three of them right in Lightning Creek, phosphorescent orange verticals of ghost fire that seemed to come and go.

In the morning, there at 177° 16′ where I'd seen the big fire was a strange brown patch in the snowy rock showing where the fire had raged and sputtered out in the all-night rain that followed the lightning. But the result of this storm was disastrous fifteen miles away at McAllister Creek where a great blaze had outlasted the rain and exploded the following afternoon in a cloud that could be seen from Seattle. I felt sorry for the fellows who had to fight these fires, the smoke-jumpers who parachuted down on them out of planes and the trail crews who hiked to them, climbing and scrambling over slippery rocks and scree slopes, arriving sweaty and exhausted only to face the wall of heat when they got there. As a lookout I had it pretty easy and only had to concentrate on reporting the exact location (by instrument findings) of every blaze I detected.

Most days, though, it was the routine that occupied me.—— Up at seven or so every day, a pot of coffee brought to a boil over a handful of burning twigs, I'd go out in the alpine yard with a cup of coffee hooked in my thumb and leisurely make my wind speed and wind direction and temperature and moisture readings — then, after chopping wood, I'd use the two-way radio and report to the relay station on Sourdough.—— At 10 A.M. I usually got hungry for breakfast, and I'd make delicious pancakes, eating them at my little table that was decorated with bouquets of mountain lupine and sprigs of fir.

Early in the afternoon was the usual time for my kick of the day, instant chocolate pudding with hot coffee.—— Around two or three I'd lie on my back on the meadowside and watch the clouds float by, or pick blueberries and eat them right there. The radio was on loud enough to hear any calls for Desolation.

Then at sunset I'd roust up my supper out of cans of yams and Spam and peas, or sometimes just pea soup with corn muffins baked on top of the wood stove in aluminum foil.—— Then I'd go out to that precipitous snow slope and shovel my two pails of snow for the water tub and gather an armful of fallen firewood from the hillside like the proverbial Old Woman of Japan.—— For the chipmunks and conies I put pans of leftovers under the shack, in the middle of the night I could hear them clanking around. The rat would scramble down from the attic and eat some too.

Sometimes I'd yell questions at the rocks and trees, and across gorges, or yodel —— "What is the meaning of the void?" The answer was perfect silence, so I knew.——

Before bedtime I'd read by kerosene lamp whatever books were in the shack.—— It's amazing how people in solitary hunger after books.—— After poring over every word of a medical tome, and the synopsized versions of Shakespeare's plays by Charles and Mary Lamb, I climbed up in the little attic and put together torn cowboy pocket books and magazines the mice had ravaged —— I also played stud poker with three imaginary players.

Around bedtime I'd bring a cup of milk almost to a boil with a tablespoon of honey in it, and drink that for my lamby nightcap, then I'd curl up in my sleeping bag.

No man should go through life without once experiencing healthy, even bored solitude in the wilderness, finding himself depending solely on himself and thereby learning his true and hidden strength.—— Learning, for instance, to eat when he's hungry and sleep when he's sleepy.

Also around bedtime was my singing time. I'd pace up and down the well-worn path in the dust of my rock singing all the show tunes I could remember, at the top of my voice too, with nobody to hear except the deer and the bear.

In the red dusk, the mountains were symphonies in pink snow —— Jack Mountain, Three Fools Peak, Freezeout Peak, Golden Horn, Mt. Terror, Mt. Fury, Mt. Despair, Crooked Thumb Peak, Mt. Challenger and the incomparable Mt. Baker bigger than the world in the distance —— and my own little Jackass Ridge that completed the Ridge of Desolation.—— Pink snow and the clouds all distant and frilly like ancient remote cities of Buddhaland splendor, and the wind working incessantly —— whish, whish —— booming, at times rattling my shack.

For supper I made chop suey and baked some biscuits and put the leftovers in a pan for deer that came in the moonlit night and nibbled like big strange cows of peace —— long-antlered buck and does and babies too —— as I meditated in the alpine grass facing the magic moon-laned lake.—— And I could see firs reflected in the moonlit lake five thousand feet below, upside down, pointing to infinity.——

And all the insects ceased in honor of the moon.

Sixty-three sunsets I saw revolve on that perpendicular hill —— mad raging sunsets pouring in sea foams of cloud through unimaginable crags like the crags you grayly drew in pencil as a child, with every rose-tint of hope beyond, making you feel just like them, brilliant and bleak beyond words.——

Cold mornings with clouds billowing out of Lightning Gorge like smoke from a giant fire but the lake cerulean as ever.

August comes in with a blast that shakes your house and augurs little Augusticity —— then that snowy-air and woodsmoke feeling —— then the snow comes sweeping your way from Canada, and the wind rises and dark low clouds rush up as out of a forge. Suddenly a green-rose rainbow appears right on your ridge with steamy clouds all around and an orange sun turmoiling . . .

> *What is a rainbow,*
> *Lord?—a hoop*
> *For the lowly*

. . . and you go out and suddenly your shadow is ringed by the rainbow as you walk on the hilltop, a lovely-haloed mystery making you want to pray.——

A blade of grass jiggling in the winds of infinity, anchored to a rock, and for your own poor gentle flesh no answer.

Your oil lamp burning in infinity.

ONE MORNING I found bear stool and signs of where the monster had taken a can of frozen milk and squeezed it in his paws and bit into it with one sharp tooth trying to suck out the paste.—— In the foggy dawn I looked down the mysterious Ridge of Starvation with its fog-lost firs and its hills humping into invisibility, and the wind blowing the fog by like a faint blizzard and I realized that somewhere in the fog stalked the bear.

And it seemed as I sat there that this was the Primordial Bear, and that he owned all the Northwest and all the snow and commanded all the mountains. —— He was King Bear, who could crush my head in his paws and crack my spine like a stick and this was his house, his yard, his domain.—— Though I looked all day, he would not show himself in the mystery of those silent foggy slopes —— he prowled at night among unknown lakes, and in the early morning the pearl-pure light that shadowed mountainsides of fir made him blink with respect.—— He had millenniums of prowling here behind him, he had seen the Indians and Redcoats come and go, and would see much more.—— He continuously heard the reassuring rapturous rush of silence, except when near creeks, he was aware of the light material the world is made of, yet he never discoursed, nor communicated by signs, nor wasted a breath complaining —— he just nibbled and pawed and lumbered along snags paying no attention to things inanimate or animate.—— His big mouth chew-chewed in the night, I could hear it across the mountain in the starlight.—— Soon he would come out of the fog, huge, and come and stare in my window with big burning eyes.—— He was Avalokitesvara the Bear, and his sign was the gray wind of autumn.——

I was waiting for him. He never came.

FINALLY THE AUTUMN RAINS, all-night gales of soaking rain as I lie warm as toast in my sleeping bag and the mornings open cold wild fall days with high wind, racing fogs, racing clouds, sudden bright sun, pristine light on hill patches and my fire crackling as I exult and sing at the top of my voice.—— Outside my window a wind-swept chipmunk sits up straight on a rock, hands clasped he nibbles an oat between his paws —— the little nutty lord of all he surveys.

Thinking of the stars night after night I begin to realize "The stars are words" and all the innumerable worlds in the Milky Way are words, and so is this world too. And I realize that no matter where I am, whether in a little room full of thought, or in this endless universe of stars and mountains, it's all in my mind.

There's no need for solitude. So love life for what it is, and form no preconceptions whatever in your mind.

WHAT STRANGE SWEET THOUGHTS come to you in the mountain solitudes!—— One night I realized that when you give people understanding and encouragement a funny little meek childish look abashes their eyes, no matter what they've been doing they weren't sure it was right —— lambies all over the world.

For when you realize that God is Everything you know that you've got to love everything no matter how bad it is, in the ultimate sense it was neither good nor bad (consider the dust), it was just *what was*, that is, what was made to appear.—— Some kind of drama to teach something to something, some "despiséd substance of divinest show."

And I realized I didnt have to hide myself in desolation but could accept society for better or for worse, like a wife —— I saw that if it wasnt for the six senses, of seeing, hearing, smelling, touching, tasting and thinking, the self of that, which is non-existent, there would be no phenomena to perceive at all, in fact no six senses or self.—— The fear of extinction is much worse than extinction (death) itself.—— To chase after extinction in the old Nirvanic sense of Buddhism is ultimately silly, as the dead indicate in the silence of their blissful sleep in Mother Earth which is an Angel hanging in orbit in Heaven anyway.——

I just lay on the mountain meadowside in the moonlight, head to grass, and heard the silent recognition of my temporary woes.—— Yes, so to try to *attain* to Nirvana when you're already there, to attain to the top of a mountain when you're already there and only have to stay —— thus, to *stay* in the Nirvana Bliss, is all I have to do, you have to do, no effort, no path really, no discipline but just to know that all is empty and awake, a Vision and a Movie in God's Universal Mind (*Alaya-Vijnana*) and to stay more or less wisely in that.—— Because silence itself is the sound of diamonds which can cut through anything, the sound of Holy Emptiness, the sound of extinction and bliss, that graveyard silence which is like the silence of an infant's smile, the sound of eternity, of the blessedness surely to be believed, the sound of nothing-ever-happened-except-God (which I'd soon hear in a noisy Atlantic tempest).—— What exists is God in His Emanation, what does not exist is God in His peaceful Neutrality, what neither exists nor does not exist is God's immortal primordial dawn of Father Sky (this world this very minute).—— So I said:—— "Stay in that, no dimensions here to any of the mountains or mosquitos and whole milky ways of worlds ——" Because sensation is emptiness, old age is emptiness.—— 'T's only the Golden Eternity of God's Mind so practise kindness and sympathy, remember that men are *not responsible in themselves as men* for their ignorance and unkindness, they should be pitied, God does pity it, because who says anything about anything since everything is just what it is, free of interpretations.—— God is not the "attainer," he is the "farer" in that which everything is, the "abider" —— one caterpillar, a thousand hairs of God.—— So know constantly that this is only you, God, empty and awake and eternally free as the unnumerable atoms of emptiness everywhere.——

I decided that when I would go back to the world down there I'd try to keep my mind clear in the midst of murky human ideas smoking like factories on the horizon through which I would walk, forward . . .

When I came down in September a cool old golden look had come into the forest, auguring cold snaps and frost and the eventual howling blizzard that would cover my shack completely, unless those winds at the top of the world would keep her bald. As I reached the bend in the trail where the shack would disappear and I would plunge down to the lake to meet the boat that would take me out and home, I turned and blessed Desolation Peak and the little pagoda on top and thanked them for the shelter and the lesson I'd been taught.

7. BIG TRIP TO EUROPE

I SAVED EVERY CENT and then suddenly I blew it all on a big glorious trip to Europe or anyplace, and I felt light and gay, too.

It took a few months but I finally bought a ticket on a Yugoslavian freighter bound from Brooklyn Busch Terminal for Tangier, Morocco.

A February morning in 1957 we sailed. I had a whole double stateroom to myself, all my books, peace, quiet and study. For once I was going to be a writer who didnt have to do other people's work.

Gastank cities of America fading beyond the waves here we go across the Atlantic now on a run that takes twelve days to Tangier that sleepy Arabic port on the other side —— and after the west waved land had receded beneath the cap lick, bang, we hit a bit of a tempest that builds up till Wednesday morning the waves are two stories high coming in over our bow and crashing over and frothing in my cabin window enough to make any old seadog duck and those poor Yugoslavian buggers out there sent to lash loose trucks and fiddle with halyards and punchy whistling lines in that salt boorapoosh gale, blam, and twasnt until later I learned these hardy Slavs had two little kittykats stashed away belowdecks and after the storm had abated (and I had seen the glowing white vision of God in my tremors of thought to think we'd might have to lower the boats away in the hopeless mess of mountainous seas —— pow pow pow the waves coming in harder and harder, higher and higher, till Wednesday morning when I looked out of my porthole from a restless try-sleep on my belly with pillows on each side of me to prevent me from pitching, I look and see a wave so immense and Jonah-like coming at me from starboard I just cant believe it, just cant believe I got on that Yugoslav freighter for my big trip to Europe at just the wrong time, just the boat that would carry me indeed to the other shore, to go join coral Hart Crane in those undersea gardens) —— the poor little kitty cats tho when the storm's abated and moon come out and looked like a dark olive prophesying Africa (O the history of the world is full of olives) here are the two little swickle jaws sitting facing each other on a calm eight o'clock hatch in the calm Popeye moonlight of the Sea Hag and finally I got them to come in my stateroom and purr on my lap as we thereafter gently swayed to the other shore, the Afric shore and not the one death'll take us to.—— But in the moment of the storm I wasnt so cocky as I am now writing about it, I was certain it was the end and I did see that everything is God, that nothing ever happened except God, the raging sea, the poor groomus lonesome boat sailing beyond every horizon with big long tortured body and with no arbitrary conception of any awakened worlds or any myriads of angel flower bearing Devas honoring the place where the

Diamond was studied, pitching like a bottle in that howling void, but soon enough the fairy hills and honey thighs of the sweethearts of Africa, the dogs, cats, chickens, Berbers, fish heads and curlylock singing keeners of the sea with its Mary star and the white house lighthouse mysterioso supine —— "What was that storm anyway?" I manage to ask by means of signs and pig English of my blond cabinboy (go up on mast be blond Pip) and he says to me only "BOORAPOOSH! BOORAPOOSHE!" with pig poosh of his lips, which later from English-speaking passenger I learn means only "North Wind," the name given for North Wind in the Adriatic.——

Only passenger on the ship beside myself is a middleaged ugly woman with glasses a Yugoslavian iron curtain Russian spy for sure sailed with me so she could study my passport in secret in the captain's cabin at night and then forge it and then finally I never gets to Tangier but am hid belowsides and taken to Yugoslavia forever nobody hears from me ever again and the only thing I dont suspect the crew of the Red ship (with her Red Star of the blood of the Russias on the stack) is of starting the tempest that almost done us in and folded us over the olive of the sea, that was how bad it was in fact then I began to have reverse paranoiac reveries that they themselves were holding conclaves in the sea sway lantern foc'sle saying "That capitalist scum American on board is a Jonah, the storm has come because of him, throw him over" so I lie there on my bunk rolling violently from side to side dreaming of how it will be with me thrun in that ocean out there (with her 80 mile an hour sprays coming off the top of waves high enough to swamp the Bank of America) how the whale if it can get to me before I drown upsidedown will indeed swallow me and leave me in its groomus dick interior to go salt me off its tip tongue on some (O God amighty) on

some cross shore in the last curlylock forbidden unknown
sea shore, I'll be laying on the beach Jonah with my
vision of the ribs —— in real life tho all it is, the sailors
werent particularly worried by the immense seas, to
them just another boorapoosh, to them just only what
they call "Veoory bod weather" and in the diningroom
there I am every evening alone at a long white table
cloth with the Russian spy woman, facing her dead
center, a Continental seating arrangement that prevents
me from relaxing in my chair and staring into space as I
eat or wait for the next course, it's tuna fish and olive
oil and olives for breakfast, it's salted fish for breakfast,
what I wouldnt have given for some peanut butter and
milkshakes I cant say.—— I canna say the Scotch neer
invented seas like that to put the mouse scare in the
hem haw roll plan —— but the pearl of the water, the
swiggin whirl, the very glisten-remembered white cap
flick in high winds, the Vision of God I had as being all
and the same myself, the ship, the others, the dreary
kitchen, the dreary slob kitchen of the sea with her
swaying pots in the gray gloom as tho the pots know
they're about to contain fish stew in the serious kitchen
below the kitchen of the serious sea, the swaying and
clank clank, O that old ship tho with all her long hull
which at first in Brooklyn dock I'd secretly thought "My
God it is too long," now is not long enough to stay still
in the immense playfulnesses of God, plowing on, plowing on and shuddering all iron —— and too after I'd
thought "Why do they have to spend a whole day here
in gastank majoun town" (in New Jersey, what's the
name, Perth Amboy) with a big black sinister I must
say hose bent in over from the gas dock pumping in and
pumping in quietly all that whole Sunday, with lowering
winter skies all orange flare crazy and nobody on the
long empty pier when I go out to walk after the olive
oil supper but one guy, my last American, walking by

looking at me a little fishy thinking I'm a member of the Red crew, pumping in all day filling those immense fuel tanks of the old *Slovenia* but once we're at sea in that God storm I'm so glad and groan to think we did spend all day loading fuel, how awful it would have been to run out of fuel in the middle of that storm and just bob there helpless turning this way and that.—— To escape the storm on that Wednesday morning for instance the captain simply turned his back to it, he could never take it from the side, only front or back, the roll-in biggies, and when he did make his turn about 8 A.M. I thought we were going to founder for sure, the whole ship with that unmistakable wrack snap went swiftly to the one side, with elastic bounce you could feel she was coming back the other way all the way, the waves from boora-poosh helped, hanging on to my porthole and looking out (not cold but spray in my face) here we go pitching over again into an upcoming sea rise and I'm looking face to face with a vertical wall of sea, the ship jerks, the keel holds, the long keel underneath that's now a little fish flapper after in the dock I'd thought "How deep these pier slips have to be hold in those long keels so they wont scrape bottom."—— Over we go, the waves wash onto the deck, my porthole and face is splashed completely, the water spills into my bed, (O my bed the sea) and over again the other way, then a steady as she goes as the captain gets the *Slovenia* around with her back to the storm and we flee south.—— Soon enough I thought we'd be deep with inward stare in an endless womb bliss, drowned —— in the grinning sea that re-stores impossibly.—— O snowy arms of God, I saw His arms there on the side of the Jacob's Ladder place where, if we had to disembark and go over (as tho life-boats would do anything but crash like splinter against the shipside in that madness) the white personal Face of God telling me "Ti Jean, dont worry, if I take you today, and all the other poor devils on this tub, it's because nothing ever happened except Me, everything is Me——" or as Lankavatara Scripture says, "There's nothing in the world but Mind itself" ("There's nothing in the world but the Golden Eternity of God's mind," I say)—— I saw the words EVERYTHING IS GOD, NOTHING EVER HAPPENED EXCEPT GOD writ in milk on that sea dip—— bless you, an endless train into an endless graveyard is all this life is, but it was never anything but God, nothing else but that—— so the higher the monstrous sinker comes fooling and calling me down names the more I shall joy old Rembrandt with my bear cup and wrassle all the Tolstoy kidders in this side of fingertwick, pluck as you will, and Afric we'll reach, and did reach anyway, and if I learned a lesson it was lesson in WHITE—— radiate all you will sweet darkness and bring ghosts and angels and so we'll put-put right along to the tree shore, the rocky shore, the final swan salt, O Ezekiel for came that afternoon so sweet and calm and Mediterranean-like when we began to see land, twasnt till I saw the keen little grin on the captain's face as he gazed through his binoculars I really believed it, but finally I could see it myself, Africa, I could see the cuts in the mountains, the dry arroyo rills before I could see the mountains themselves and finally did see them, pale green gold, not knowing till about 5 they were really the mountains of Spain, old Hercules was somewhere up there ahead holding up the world on his shoulders thus the hush and glassy silence of these entry waters to Hesperid.—— Sweet Mary star ahead, and all the rest, and further on too I could see Paris, my big kleig light vision Paris where I'd go get off a train at outside town Peuples du Pais, and walk 5 miles deeper and deeper as in a dream into the city of Paris itself arriving finally at some golden center of it I envisioned then, which was silly, as it turned out, as tho Paris had a center.—— Faint little white dots at the foot of the long green Africa mountain and yessiree that was the sleepy little Arab city of Tangier waiting for me to explore it that night so I go down into my stateroom and keep checking my rucksack to see it's well packed and ready for me to swing down the gangplank with and get my passport stamped with Arabic figures "Oieieh eiieh ekkei."—— Meanwhile a lot of trade going by, boats, several beat Spanish freighters you couldnt believe so beat, bleak, small, that have to face boorapooshes with nothing but half our length and half our girth and over there the long stretches of sand on the shore of Spain indicative of dryer Cadizes that I had dreamed yet I still insisted on dreaming of the Spanish cape, the Spanish star, the Spanish gutter song.—— And finally one amazing little Moroccan fishingboat putting out to sea with a small crew of about five, in sloppy Catch-Mohammed pants some of them (balloony pantaloons they wear in case they give birth to Mohammed) and some with red fezzes but red fezzes like you never thought they'd be real fezzes with wow grease and creases and dust on them, real red fezzes of real life in real Africa the wind blowing and the little fishing sloop with its incredible high poop made of Lebanon wood —— putting out to the curlylock song of the sea, the stars all night, the nets, the twang of Ramadan . . .

OF COURSE WORLD TRAVEL isn't as good as it seems, it's only after you've come back from all the heat and horror that you forget to get bugged and remember the weird scenes you saw.—— In Morocco I went for a walk one beautiful cool sunny afternoon (with breeze from Gibraltar) and my friend and I walked to the outskirts of the weird Arab town commenting on the architecture, the furniture, the people, the sky which he said would look green at nightfall and the quality of the food in the various restaurants around town, adding, he did, "Besides I'm just a hidden agent from another planet and the trouble is I dont know why they sent me, I've forgotten the goddam message dearies" so I says "I'm a messenger from heaven too" and suddenly we saw a herd of goats coming down the road and behind it an Arab shepherd boy of ten who held a little baby lamb in his arms and behind him came the mother lamb bleating and baa haa ing for him to take real good extryspecial care of the babe, which the boy said "Egraya fa y kapata katapatafataya" and spat it out of his throat in the way Semites speak.—— I said "Look, a real shepherd boy carrying a baby lamb!" and Bill said: "O well, the little prigs are always rushing around carrying lambs." Then we walked down the hill to a place where a holy man or that is, a devout Mohammedan, kneeled praying to the setting sun towards Mecca and Bill turned to me and said: "Wouldnt it be wonderful if we were real American tourists and I suddenly rushed up with a camera to snap his picture?" . . . then added: "By the way, how do we walk around him?"

"Around his right," I said anyway.

We wended our way homeward to the chatty outdoor cafe where all the people gathered at nightfall beneath screaming trees of birds, near the Zoco Grande, and decided to follow the railroad track. It was hot but the breeze was cool from the Mediterranean. We came to an old Arab hobo sitting on the rail of the track recounting the Koran to a bunch of raggedy children listening attentively or at least obediently. Behind them was their mother's house, a tin hut, there she was in white hanging white and blue and pink wash in front of a pale blue tin hovel in the bright African sun.—— I didnt know what the holy man was doing, I said "He's an idiot of some kind?"——"No," says Bill, "he's a wandering Sherifian pilgrim preaching the gospel of Allah to the children—— he's a *hombre que rison*, a man who prays, they got some *hombres que rison* in town that wear white robes and go around barefoot in the alleys and dont let no bluejeaned hoodlums start a fight on the street, he just walks up and stares at them and they scat. Besides, the people of Tangiers aint like the people of West Side New York, when there's a fight starts in the street among the Arab hoods all the men rush up out of mint tea shops and beat the shit out of them. They aint got men in America any more, they just sit there and eat pizzas before the late show, my dear." This man was William Seward Burroughs, the writer, and we were heading now down the narrow alleys of the Medina (the "Casbah" is only the Fort part of town) to a little bar and restaurant where all the Americans and exiles went. I wanted to tell somebody about the shepherd boy, the holy man and the man on the tracks but no one was interested. The big fat Dutch owner of the bar said "I cant find a good poy in this town" (saying "poy," not boy, but meaning boy).—— Burroughs doubled up in laughter.

We went from there to the late afternoon cafe where sat all the decayed aristocrats of America and Europe and a few eager enlightened healthy Arabs or near-Arabs or diplomats or whatever they were.—— I said to Bill: "Where do I get a woman in this town?"

He said: "There's a few whores that hang around, you have to know a cabdriver or something, or better than that there's a cat here in town, from Frisco, Jim, he'll show you what corner and what to do" so that night me and Jim the painter go out and stand on the corner and sure enough here come two veiled women, with delicate cotton veil over their mouths and halfway up their noses, just their dark eyes you see, and wearing long flowing robes and you see their shoes cuttin through the robes and Jim hailed a cab which was waiting there and off we went to the pad which was a patio affair (mine) with tile patio overlooking the sea and a Sherifian beacon that turned on and turned on, around and around, flashing in my window every now and again, as, alone with one of the mysterious shrouds, I watched her flip off the shroud and veil and saw standing there a perfect little Mexican (or that is to say Arab) beauty perfect and brown as ye old October grapes and maybe like the wood of Ebon and turned to me with her lips parted in curious "Well what are you doing standing there?" so I lighted a candle on my desk. When she left she went downstairs with me where some of my connections from England and Morocco and U.S.A. were all blasting home made pipes of Opium and singing Cab Calloway's old tune, "I'm gonna kick the gong around."—— On the street she was very polite when she got into the cab.

From there I went to Paris later, where nothing much happened except the most beautiful girl in the world who didnt like my rucksack on my back and had a date anyway with a guy with a small mustache who stands hand in sidepocket with a sneer in the nightclub movies of Paris.

Wow —— and in London what do I see but a beautiful, a heavenly beautiful blonde standing against a wall in Soho calling out to welldressed men. Lots of makeup, with blue eye shadow, the most beautiful women in the world are definitely English ... unless like me you like em dark.

BUT THERE WAS MORE TO MOROCCO than walks with Burroughs and whores in my room, I took long hikes by myself, sipped Cinzano at sidewalk cafes *solitaire,* sat on the beach ...

There was a railroad track on the beach that brought the train from Casablanca —— I used to sit in the sand watching the weird Arab brakemen and their funny little CFM Railroad (Central Ferrocarril Morocco). —— The cars had thin spoked wheels, just bumpers instead of couplings, double cylindrical bumpers each side, and the cars were tied on by means of a simple chain.—— The tagman signalled with ordinary stop-hand and go-ahead goose and had a thin piercing whistle and screamed in Arabic spitting-from-the-throat to the rear man.—— The cars had no handbrakes and no rung ladders.—— Weird Arab bums sat in coal hoppers being switched up and down the sandy seashore, expecting to go to Tetuan . . .

One brakeman wore a fez and balloon pantaloons —— I could just picture the dispatcher in a full Jalaba robe sitting with his pipe of hasheesh by the phone.—— But they had a good Diesel switch engine with a fezzed hoghead inside at the throttle and a sign on the side of the engine that said DANGER A MORT (danger unto death).—— Instead of handbrakes they ran rushing in flowing robes and released a horizontal bar that braked the wheels with brake shoes —— it was insane —— they were miraculous railroad men.—— The tagman ran yelling "Thea! Thea! Mohammed! Thea!"—— Mohammed was the head man, he stood up at the far end of the sand gazing sadly.—— Meanwhile veiled Arab women in long Jesus robes walked around picking up bits of coal by the tracks —— for the night's fish, the night's heat.—— But the sand, the rails, the grass, was as universal as old Southern Pacific. . . . White robes by the blue sea railroad bird sand . . .

I had a very nice room as I say on the roof, with a patio, the stars at night, the sea, the silence, the French landlady, the Chinese housekeeper —— the six foot seven Hollander pederast who lived next door and brought Arab boys up every night.—— Nobody bothered me.

145

The ferry boat from Tangier to Algeciras was very sad because it was all lit up so gayly for the terrible business of going to the other shore.——

In the Medina I found a hidden Spanish restaurant serving the following menu for 35 cents: one glass red wine, shrimp soup with little noodles, pork with red tomato sauce, bread, one egg fried, one orange on a saucer and one black espresso coffee: I swear on my arm.——

For the business of writing and sleeping and thinking I went to the local cool drugstore and bought Sympatina for excitement, Diosan for the codeine dream, and Soneryl for sleep.—— Meanwhile Burroughs and I also got some opium from a guy in a red fez in the Zoco Chico and made some home made pipes with old olive oil cans and smoked singing "Willie the Moocher" and the next day mixed hash and kif with honey and spices and made big "Majoun" cakes and ate them, chewing, with hot tea, and went on long prophetic walks to the fields of little white flowers.—— One afternoon high on hasheesh I meditated on my sun roof thinking "All things that move are God, and all things that dont move are God" and at this re-utterance of the ancient secret all things that moved and made noise in the Tangier afternoon seemed to suddenly rejoice, and all things that didnt move seemed pleased . . .

Tangier is a charming, cool, nice city, full of marvelous Continental restaurants like *El Paname* and *L'Escargot* with mouth-watering cuisine, sweet sleeps, sunshine, and galleries of holy Catholic priests near where I lived who prayed to the seaward every evening.—— Let there be orisons everywhere!——

Meanwhile mad genius Burroughs sat typing wild-haired in his garden apartment the following words: —— "Motel Motel Motel loneliness moans across the continent like fog over still oily water tidal rivers . . ."

146

(meaning America.) (America's always rememberable in exile.)

On Moroccan Independence Day my big 50-year-old sexy Arab Negress maid cleaned my room and folded my filthy unwashed T-shirt neatly on a chair . . .

And yet sometimes Tangier was unutterably dull, no vibrations, so I'd walk two miles along the beach among the ancient rhythmic fishermen who hauled nets in singing gangs with some ancient song along the surf, leaving the fish slopping in sea-eye sand, and sometimes I'd watch the terrific soccer games being played by mad Arab boys in the sand some of them throwing in scores with backward tosses of their heads to applause of galleries of children.——

And I'd walk the Maghreb Land of huts which is as lovely as the land of old Mexico with all those green hills, burros, old trees, gardens.——

One afternoon I sat in a riverbottom that fed into the sea and watched the high tide swelling in higher than my head and a sudden rainstorm got me to running back along the beach to town like a trotting track star, soaked, then suddenly on the boulevard of cafes and hotels the sun came out and illuminated the wet palm trees and it gave me an old feeling —— I had that old feeling —— I thought of everybody.

Weird town. I sat in the Zoco Chico at a cafe table watching the types go by: A weird Sunday in Fellaheen Arabland with you'd expect mystery white windows and ladies throwing daggers and do see but by God the woman up there I saw in a white veil sitting and peering by a Red Cross above a little sign that said: —— "Practicantes, Sanio Permanente, TF No. 卐 9766" the cross being red —— right over a tobacco shop with luggage and pictures, where a little barelegged boy leaned on a counter with a family of wristwatched Spaniards.—— Meanwhile English sailors from the submarines passed

trying to get drunker and drunker on Malaga yet quiet
and lost in home regret.—— Two little Arab hepcats had
a brief musical confab (boys of ten) and then parted
with a push of arms and wheeling of arms, one boy had
a yellow skullcap and a blue zoot suit.—— The black
and white tiles of the outdoor cafe where I sat were
soiled by lonely Tangier time —— a little baldcropped
boy walked by, went to a man at a table near me, said
"Yo" and the waiter rushed up and scatted him off
shouting "Yig."—— A brown ragged robe priest sat
with me at a table (an *hombre que rison*) but looked off
with hands on lap at brilliant red fez and red girl
sweater and red boy shirt green scene . . . Dreaming of
Sufi . . .

Oh the poems that a Catholic will get in an Islam
Land: —— "Holy Sherifian Mother blinking by the
black sea . . . did you save the Phoenecians drowning
three thousand years ago? . . . O soft queen of the midnight horses. . . . bless the Marocaine rough lands!" . . .

For they were suren hell rough lands and I found
out one day by climbing way up into the back hills.——
First I went down the coast, in the sand, where the sea-
gulls all together in a group by the sea were like having
a refection at table, a shiny table —— at first I thought
they were praying —— the head gull said grace.——
Sitting in the sea side sand I wondered if the microscopic
red bugs in it ever met and mated.—— I tried to count
a pinch of sand knowing there are as many worlds as the
sands in all the oceans.—— O honored of the worlds!
for just then an old robed Bodhisattva, an old robed
bearded realizer of the greatness of wisdom came walking by with a staff and a shapeless skin bag and a cotton
pack and a basket on his back, with white cloth around his
hoary brown brow.—— I saw him coming from miles
away down the beach —— the shrouded Arab by the

148

sea.—— We didnt even nod to each other —— it was too much, we'd known each other too long ago ——

After that I climbed inland and reached a mountain overlooking all Tangier Bay and came to a quiet shepherd slope, ah the honk of asses and maaaa of sheep up there rejoicing in Vales, and the silly happy trills of crazybirds goofing in the solitude of rocks and brush swept by sun heat swept by sea wind, and all the warm ululations shimmering.—— Quiet brush-and-twig huts looking like Upper Nepal.—— Fierce looking Arab shepherds went by scowling at me, dark, bearded, robed, bare knee'd.—— To the South were the distant African mountains.—— Below me on the steep slope where I sat were quiet powder blue villages.—— Crickets, sea roar.—— Peaceful mountain Berber Villages or farm settlements, women with huge bundles of twigs on their backs going down the hill —— little girls among browsing bulls.—— Dry arroyos in the fat green meadowland. —— And the Carthaginians have disappeared?

When I went down back to the beach in front of Tangier White City it was night and I looked at the hill where I lived all be-sparkled, and thought, "And I live up there full of imaginary conceptions?"

The Arabs were having their Saturday night parade with bagpipes, drums and trumpets: it put me in the mind of a Haiku: ——

> Walking along the night beach
> —— Military music
> On the boulevard.

SUDDENLY ONE NIGHT IN TANGIER where as I say I'd been somewhat bored, a lovely flute began to blow around three o'clock in the morning, and muffled

drums beat somewhere in the depths of the Medina.——
I could hear the sounds from my sea-facing room in the
Spanish quarter, but when I went out on my tiled terrace there was nothing there but a sleeping Spanish
dog.—— The sounds came from blocks away, toward the
markets, under the Mohammedan stars.—— It was the
beginning of Ramadan, the month-long fast. How sad:
because Mohammed had fasted from sunrise to sun-
down, a whole world would too because of belief under
these stars.—— Out on the other crook of the bay the
beacon turned and sent its shaft into my terrace (twenty
dollars a month), swung around and swept the Berber
hills where weirder flutes and stranger deeper drums
were blowing, and out into the mouth of the Hesperides
in the softing dark that leads to the dawn off the coast
of Africa.—— I suddenly felt sorry that I had already
bought my boat ticket to Marseille and was leaving
Tangier.

If you ever take the packet from Tangier to Marseille never go fourth-class.—— I thought I was such a
clever world-weary traveler and saving five dollars, but
when I got on the packet the following morning at
7 A.M. (a great blue shapeless hulk that had looked so
romantic to me steaming around the little Tangier jetty
from down-the-coast Casablanca) I was instantly told
to wait with a gang of Arabs and then after a half hour
herded down into the fo'c'sle —— a French Army bar-
racks. All the bunks were occupied so I had to sit on
the deck and wait another hour. After a few desultory
explorations among the stewards I was told that I had
not been assigned a bunk and that no arrangements had
been made to feed me or anything. I was practically a
stowaway. Finally I saw a bunk no one seemed to be
using and appropriated it, angrily asking the soldier
nearby, *"Ill y a quelqu'un ici?"* He didnt even bother
to answer, just gave me a shrug, not necessarily a Gallic

shrug but a great world-weary life-weary shrug of Europe in general. I was suddenly sorry I was leaving the rather listless but earnest sincerity of the Arab world.

The silly tub took off across the Strait of Gibraltar and immediately began to pitch furiously in the long ground swells, probably the worst in the world, that take place off the rock bottom of Spain.—— It was almost noon by now.—— After a short meditation on the burlap-covered bunk I went out to the deck where the soldiers were scheduled to line up with their ration plates, and already half the French Army had regurgitated on the deck and it was impossible to walk across it without slipping.—— Meanwhile I noticed that even the third-class passengers had dinner set out for them in their dining room and that they had rooms and service.—— I went back to my bunk and pulled out my old camp pack equipment, an aluminum pot and cup and spoon from my rucksack, and waited.—— The Arabs were still sitting on the floor.—— The big fat German chief steward, looking like a Prussian bodyguard, came in and announced to the French troops fresh from duty on the hot borders of Algeria to snap to it and do a cleaning job.—— They stared at him silently and he went away with his retinue of ratty stewards.

At noon everybody began to stir about and even sing.—— I saw the soldiers straggling forward with their pans and spoons and followed them, then advanced with the line to a dirty kitchen pot full of plain boiled beans which were slopped into my pot after a desultory glance from the scullion who wondered why my pot looked a little different.—— But to make the meal a success I went to the bakery in the bow and gave the fat baker, a Frenchman with a mustache, a tip, and he gave me a beautiful oven-fresh little loaf of bread and with this I sat on a coil of rope on the bow hatch and ate in the clean winds and actually enjoyed the meal.—— Off to the portside Gibraltar rock was already receding, the waters were getting calmer, and soon it would be lazy afternoon with the ship well into the route toward Sardinia and southern France.—— And suddenly (as I had had such long daydreams about this trip, all ruined now, of a beautiful glittering voyage on a magnificent "packet" with red wine in thin-stemmed glasses and jolly Frenchmen and blondes) a little hint of what I was looking for in France (to which I'd never been) came over the public-address system: a song called *Mademoiselle de Paris* and all the French soldiers on the bow with me sitting protected against the wind behind bulkheads and housings suddenly got romantic-looking and began to talk heatedly about their girls at home and everything suddenly seemed to point to Paris at last.

I RESOLVED TO WALK FROM MARSEILLE up on Route N8 toward Aix-en-Provence and then start hitchhiking. I never dreamed that Marseille was such a big town. After getting my passport stamped I strode across the rail yards, pack on back. The first European I greeted on his home soil was an old handlebar-mustached Frenchman who crossed the tracks with me, but he did not return my happy greeting, *"Allo l'Père!"* —— But that was all right, the very cobbles and trolley tracks were paradise for me, the ungraspable springtime France at last. I walked along, among those 18th Century smokepot tenements spouting coal smoke, passing a huge garbage wagon with a great work horse and the driver in a beret and striped polo shirt.—— An old 1929 Ford suddenly rattled by toward the water front containing four bereted toughs with butts in mouth like characters in some forgotten French movie of my mind. —— I went to a kind of bar that was open early Sunday morning where I sat at a table and drank hot coffee

served by a dame in her bathrobe, though no pastries
—— but I got them across the street in the *boulangerie*
smelling of crisp fresh Napoleons and *croissants*, and
ate heartily while reading *Paris Soir* and with the music
on the radio already announcing news of my eagered-
for Paris —— sitting there with inexplicable tugging
memories as though I'd been born before and lived before in this town, been brothers with someone, and bare
trees fuzzing green for spring as I looked out of the
window.—— How old my old life in France, my long
old Frenchness, seemed —— all those names of the shops,
épicerie, *boucherie*, the early-morning little stores like
those of my French-Canadian home, like Lowell Massachusetts on a Sunday.—— *Quel différence?* I was very
happy suddenly.

MY PLAN, SEEING THE LARGENESS of the
city, was to take a bus to Aix and the road north to
Avignon and Lyon and Dijon and Sens and Paris, and
I figured that tonight I would sleep in the grass of
Provence in my sleeping bag, but it turned out different.—— The bus was marvelous, it was just a local
bus and went climbing out of Marseille through tiny
communities where you'd see little French fathers put-
tering in neat gardens as their children came in the
front door with long loaves of bread for breakfast, and
the characters that got on and off the bus were so familiar I wished my folks had been there to see them,
hear them say, *"Bonjour, Madame Dubois. Vous avez
été à la Messe?"* It didnt take long to get to Aix-en-
Provence where I sat at a sidewalk café over a couple
of vermouths and watched Cézanne's trees and the gay
French Sunday: a man going by with pastries and two-
yard-long breads and sprinkled around the horizon the
dull-red rooftops and distant blue-haze hills attesting

to Cézanne's perfect reproduction of the Provençal color, a red he used even in still-life apples, a brown red, and backgrounds of dark smokeblue.—— I thought "The gaiety, the sensibleness of France is so good after the moroseness of the Arabs."

After the vermouths I went to the Cathedral of St. Sauveur, which was just a shortcut to the highway, and there passing an old man with white hair and beret (and all around on the horizon Cézanne's springtime "green" which I had forgotten went with his smoky-blue hills and rust-red roof) I cried.—— I cried in the Cathedral of the Savior to hear the choir boys sing a gorgeous old thing, while angels seemed to be hovering around —— I couldn't help myself —— I hid behind a pillar from the occasional inquiring eyes of French families on my huge rucksack (eighty pounds) and wiped my eyes, crying even at the sight of the 6th Century Baptistery —— all old Romanesque stones with the hole in the ground still, where so many other infants had been baptized all with eyes of lucid liquid diamond understanding.

I LEFT THE CHURCH and headed for the road, walked about a mile, disdaining to hitchhike at first, and finally sat by the side of the road on a grassy hill overlooking a pure Cézanne landscape —— little farm roofs and trees and distant blue hills with the suggestions of the type of cliff that is more predominant northward toward Van Gogh's country at Arles.—— The highway was full of small cars with no room or cyclists with their hair blowing.—— I trudged and thumbed hopelessly for five miles, then gave it up at Eguilles, the first bus stop on the highway, there was no hitchhiking in France I could see.—— At a rather expensive café in Eguilles, with French families dining in the open patio,

I had coffee and then knowing the bus would come in about an hour, went strolling down a country dirt road to examine the inner view of Cézanne's country and found a mauve-tan farmhouse in a quiet fertile rich valley —— rustic, with weathered pink-powder roof tiles, a gray-green mild warmness, voices of girls, gray stacks of baled hay, a fertilized chalky garden, a cherry tree in white bloom, a rooster crowing at midday mildly, tall "Cézanne" trees in back, apple trees, pussywillows in the meadow in the clover, an orchard, an old blue wagon under the barn port, a pile of wood, a dry white-twig fence near the kitchen.

Then the bus came and we went through the Arles country and now I saw the restless afternoon trees of Van Gogh in the high mistral wind, the cypress rows tossing, yellow tulips in window boxes, a vast outdoor café with huge awning, and the gold sunlight.—— I saw, understood, Van Gogh, the bleak cliffs beyond. . . . At Avignon I got off to transfer to the Paris Express. I bought my ticket to Paris but had hours to wait and wandered down in late afternoon along the main drag —— thousands of people in Sunday best on their dreary interminable provincial stroll.

I strolled into a museum full of stone carvings from the days of Pope Benedict XIII, including one splendid woodcarving showing the Last Supper with bunched Apostles grieving head-to-head, Christ in the middle, hand up, and suddenly one of the bunched heads in deeper-in relief is staring right at you and it is Judas! —— Farther down the aisle one pre-Roman, apparently Celtic monster, all old carved stone.—— And then out in the cobblestoned back-alley of Avignon (city of dust), alleys dirtier than Mexico slums (like New England streets near the dump in the Thirties), with women's shoes in gutters running with medieval slop water, and all along the stone wall raggedy children playing in forlorn swirls of mistral dust, enough to make Van Gogh weep.——

And the famous much-sung bridge of Avignon, stone, half-gone now in the spring-rushing Rhône, with medieval-walled castles on the horizon hills (for tourists now, once the baronial castle-supporter of the town). —— Sort of juvenile delinquents lurking in the Sunday afternoon dust by the Avignon wall smoking forbidden butts, girls of thirteen smirking in high heels, and down the street a little child playing in the watery gutter with the skeleton of a doll, bonging on his upturned tub for a beat.—— And old cathedrals in the alleys of town, old churches now just crumbling relics.

Nowhere in the world is as dismal as Sunday afternoon with the mistral wind blowing in the cobbled back streets of poor old Avignon. When I sat in a café in the main street reading the papers, I understood the complaint of French poets about provincialism, the dreary provincialism that drove Flaubert and Rimbaud mad and made Balzac muse.

Not one beautiful girl to be seen in Avignon except in that café, and she a sensational slender rose in dark glasses confiding love affairs to her girl friend at the table next to mine, and outside the multitudes roamed up and down, up and down, back and forth, nowhere to go, nothing to do —— Madame Bovary is wringing her hands in despair behind lace curtains, Genêt's heroes are waiting for the night, the De Musset youth is buying a ticket for the train to Paris.—— What can you do in Avignon on a Sunday afternoon? Sit in a café and read about the comeback of a local clown, sip your vermouth, and meditate the carved stone in the museum.

But I did have one of the best five-course meals in all Europe in what appeared to be a "cheap" side-street restaurant: good vegetable soup, an exquisite omelet, broiled hare, wonderful mashed potatoes (mashed through a strainer with lots of butter), a half bottle of red wine and bread and then a delicious flan with syrup, all for supposedly ninety-five cents, but the waitress raised the price from 380 francs to 575 as I ate and I didn't bother to contest the bill.

In the railroad station I stuck fifty francs into the gum machine, which didnt give, and all the officials most flagrantly passed the buck (*"Demandez au contrôleur!"*) and (*"Le contrôleur ne s'occupe pas de çà!"*) and I became somewhat discouraged by the dishonesty of France, which I'd noticed at once on that hellship packet especially after the honest religiousness of the Moslems.—— Now a train stopped, southbound to Marseille, and an old woman in black lace stepped out and walked along and soon dropped one of her black leather gloves and a well-dressed Frenchman rushed up and picked up the glove and dutifully laid it on a post so that I had to grab the glove and run after her and give it to her.—— I knew then why it is the French who perfected the guillotine —— not the English, not the Germans, not the Danes, not the Italians and not the Indians, but the French my own people.

To cap it all, when the train came there were absolutely no seats and I had to ride all night in the cold vestibule.—— When I got sleepy I had to flatten my rucksack on the cold-iron vestibule doors and I lay there curled, legs up, as we rushed through the unseen Provences and Burgundys of the gnashing French map. —— Six thousand francs for this great privilege.

ALL BUT IN THE MORNING, the suburbs of Paris, the dawn spreading over the moody Seine (like a little canal), the boats on the river, the outer industrial smokes of the city, then the Gare de Lyon and when I stepped

out on Boulevard Diderot I thought seeing one glimpse
of long boulevards leading every direction with great
eight-story ornate apartments with monarchial façades,
"Yes, they made themselves a *city!*"—— Then crossing
Boulevard Diderot to have coffee, good *espresso* coffee
and *croissants* in a big city place full of workingmen,
and through the glass I could see women in full long
dresses rushing to work on motorbikes, and men with
silly crash helmets (*La Sporting France*), taxis, broad
old cobblestoned streets, and that nameless city smell
of coffee, antiseptics and wine.

Walking, thence, in a cold brisk-red morning, over
the Austerlitz Bridge, past the Zoo on the Quai St.-
Bernard where one little old deer stood in the morning
dew, then past the Sorbonne, and my first sight of Notre
Dame strange as a lost dream.—— And when I saw a
big rimed woman statue on Boulevard St.-Germain I
remembered my dream that I was once a French school-
boy in Paris.—— I stopped at a café, ordered Cinzano,
and realized the racket of going-to-work was the same
here as in Houston or in Boston and no better —— but
I felt a vast promise, endless streets, streets, girls, places,
meanings, and I could understand why Americans stayed
here, some for lifetimes.—— And the first man in Paris
I had looked at in the Gare de Lyon was a dignified
Negro in a Homburg.

What endless human types passed my café table:
old French ladies, Malay girls, schoolboys, blond boys
going to college, tall young brunettes headed for the
law classes, hippy pimply secretaries, bereted goggled
clerks, bereted scarved carriers of milk bottles, dikes
in long blue laboratory coats, frowning older students
striding in trench coats like in Boston, seedy little cops
(in blue caps) fishing through their pockets, cute pony-
tailed blondes in high heels with zip notebooks, goggled
bicyclists with motors attached to the rear of their cycles,

bespectacled Homburgs walking around reading *Le Parisien* and breathing mist, bushyheaded mulattoes with long cigarettes in their mouths, old ladies carrying milk cans and shopping bags, rummy W. C. Fieldses spitting in the gutter and with hands-a-pockets going to their shops for another day, a young Chinese-looking French girl of twelve with separated teeth almost in tears (frowning, and with a bruise on her shin, schoolbooks in hand, cute and serious like Negro girls in Greenwich Village), porkpie executive running and catching his bus sensationally and vanishing with it, mustachioed longhaired Italian youths coming in the bar for their morning shot of wine, huge bumbling bankers of the Bourse in expensive suits fishing for newspaper pennies in their palms (bumping into women at the bus stop), serious thinkers with pipes and packages, a lovely redhead with dark glasses trotting pip pip on her heels to the bus, and a waitress slopping mop water in the gutter.——

Ravishing brunettes with tight-fitting skirts. Schoolgirlies with long boyish bobs plirping lips over books and memorizing lessons fidgetly (waiting to meet young Marcel Proust in the park after school), lovely young girls of seventeen walking with low-heeled sure strides in long red coats to downtown Paris.—— An apparent East Indian, whistling, leading a dog on a leash.—— Serious young lovers, boy arming girl's shoulders.—— Statue of Danton pointing nowhere, Paris hepcat in dark glasses faintly mustached waiting there.—— Little suited boy in black beret, with well-off father going to morning joys.

The next day I strolled down Boulevard St.-Germain in a spring wind, turned in at the church of St.-Thomas-d'Aquin and saw a huge gloomy painting on the wall showing a warrior, fallen off his horse, being stabbed in the heart by an enemy, at whom he looked directly with sad understanding Gallic eyes and one hand outheld as if to say, "It's my life" (it had that Delacroix horror). I meditated on this painting in the bright colorful Champs-Élysées and watched the multitudes go by. Glum I walked past a movie house advertising *War and Peace*, where two Russian-sabered sablecaped grenadiers chatted amiably and in French come-on with two American women tourists.

Long walks down the boulevards with a flask of cognac.—— Each night a different room, each day four hours to find a room, on foot with full pack.—— In the skid-row sections of Paris numerous frowsy dames said *"complet"* coldly when I asked for unheated cockroach rooms in the gray Paris gloom.—— I walked and hurried angrily bumping people along the Seine.—— In little cafés I had compensatory steaks and wine, chewing slowly.

Noon, a café near Les Halles, onion soup, *pâté de maison* and bread, for a quarter.—— Afternoon, the girls in fur coats along Boulevard St.-Denis, perfumed.—— *"Monsieur?"*

"Sure. . . ."

Finally I found a room I could keep for all of three days, a dismal dirty cold hovel hotel run by two Turkish pimps but the kindest fellows I'd met yet in Paris. Here, window open to dreary rains of April, I slept my best sleeps and gathered strength for daily twenty-mile hikes around the Queen of Cities.

But the next day I was suddenly unaccountably happy as I sat in the park in front of Trinité Church near Gare St.-Lazare among children and then went inside and saw a mother praying with a devotion that startled her son.—— A moment later I saw a tiny mother with a barelegged little son already as tall as she.

I walked around, it started to sleet on Pigalle, suddenly the sun broke out on Rochechouart and I discovered Montmartre.—— Now I knew where I would live if I ever came back to Paris.—— Carousels for children, marvelous markets, *hors d'oeuvres* stalls, wine-barrel stores, cafés at the foot of the magnificent white Sacré-Coeur basilica, lines of women and children waiting for hot German crullers, new Norman cider inside. —— Beautiful girls coming home from parochial school. —— A place to get married and raise a family, narrow happy streets full of children carrying long loaves of bread.—— For a quarter I bought a huge chunk of Gruyère cheese from a stall, then a huge chunk of jellied meat delicious as crime, then in a bar a quiet glass of port, and then I went to see the church high on the cliff looking down on the rain-wet roofs of Paris.——

La Basilique du Sacré-Coeur de Jésus is beauteous, maybe in its way one of the most beautiful of all churches (if you have a rococo soul as I have): blood-red crosses in the stainedglass windows with a westerly sun sending golden shafts against opposite bizarre Byzantine blues representing other sacristies —— regular blood baths in the blue sea —— and all the poor sad plaques commemorating the building of the church after the sack by Bismarck.

Down the hill in the rain, I went to a magnificent restaurant on Rue de Clignancourt and had that unbeatable French puréed soup and a whole meal with a basket of French bread and my wine and the thin-stemmed glasses I had dreamed about.—— Looking across the restaurant at the shy thighs of a newlywed girl having her big honeymoon supper with her young farmer husband, neither of them saying anything.—— Fifty years of this they'd do now in some provincial kitchen or dining room.—— The sun breaking through again, and with full belly I wandered among the shooting galleries and carousels of Montmartre and I saw a young mother hugging her little girlie with a doll, bouncing her and laughing and hugging her because they had had so much fun on the hobbyhorse and I saw Dostoevski's divine love in her eyes (and above on the hill over Montmartre, He held out His arms).

Feeling wonderful now, I strolled about and cashed a traveler's check at the Gare du Nord and walked all the way, gay and fine, down Boulevard de Magenta to the huge Place de la République and on down, cutting sometimes into side streets.—— Night now, down Boulevard du Temple and Avenue Voltaire (peeking into windows of obscure Breton restaurants) to Boulevard Beaumarchais where I thought I'd see the gloomy Bastille prison but I didn't even know it was torn down in 1789 and asked a guy, *"Où est la vieille prison de la Révolution?"* and he laughed and told me there were a few remnant stones in the subway station.—— Then down in the subway: amazing clean artistic ads, imagine an ad for wine in America showing a naked ten-year-old girl with a party hat coiled around a bottle of wine.—— And the amazing map that lights up and shows your route in colored buttons when you press the destination button.—— Imagine the New York I.R.T. And the clean trains, a bum on a bench in a clean surrealistic atmosphere (not to be compared with the 14th Street stop on the Canarsie line).

Paris paddywagons flew by singing *dee* da, *dee* da.——

The next day I strolled examining bookstores and went into the Benjamin Franklin Library, the site of the old Café Voltaire (facing the Comédie Française) where everybody from Voltaire to Gauguin to Scott Fitzgerald drank and now the scene of prim American librarians with no expression.—— Then I strolled to the Pantheon and had delicious pea soup and a small steak in a fine crowded restaurant full of students and vegetarian law professors.—— Then I sat in a little park in Place Paul-Painlevé and dreamily watched a curving row of beautiful rosy tulips rigid and swaying fat shaggy sparrows, beautiful short-haired *mademoiselles* strolling by. It's not that French girls are beautiful, it's their cute mouths and the sweet way they talk French (their mouths pout rosily), the way they've perfected the short haircut and the way they amble slowly when they walk, with great sophistication, and of course their chic way of dressing and undressing.

Paris, a stab in the heart finally.

THE LOUVRE —— MILES AND MILES of hiking before great canvases.

In David's immense canvas of Napoleon I and Pius VII I could see little altar boys far in the back fondling a *maréchal's* sword hilt (the scene is Nôtre-Dame-de-Paris, with the Empress Josephine kneeling pretty as a boulevard girl). Fragonard, so delicate next to Van Dyck, and a big smoky Rubens (*La Mort de Dido*).—— But the Rubens got better as I looked, the muscle tones in cream and pink, the rimshot luminous eyes, the dull purple velvet robe on the bed. Rubens was happy because nobody was posing for him for a fee and his gay *Kermesse* showed an old drunk about to be sick.—— Goya's *Marquesa de la Solana* could hardly have been more modern, her silver fat shoes pointed like fish crisscrossed, the immense diaphanous pink ribbons over a sisterly pink face.—— A typical French woman (not educated) suddenly said, "*Ah, c'est trop beau!*" "It's too beautiful!"

But Brueghel, wow! His *Battle of Arbelles* had at least 600 faces clearly defined in an impossibly confused mad battle leading nowhere.—— No wonder Céline loved him.—— A complete understanding of world madness, thousands of clearly defined figures with swords and above them the calm mountains, trees on a hill, clouds, and everyone laughed when they saw that insane masterpiece that afternoon, they knew what it meant.

And Rembrandt.—— The dim trees in the darkness of crépuscule château with its hints of a Transylvanian vampire castle.—— Set side by side with this his *Hanging Beef* was completely modern with its splash of blood paint. Rembrandt's brushstroke swirled in the face of the *Christ at Emmaus,* and the floor in *Sainte Famille* was completely detailed in the color of planks and nails.—— Why should anyone paint after Rembrandt, unless Van Gogh? The *Philosopher in Meditation* was my favorite for its Beethoven shadows and light, I liked also *Hermit Reading* with his soft old brow, and *St. Matthew Being Inspired by the Angel* was a miracle —— the rough strokes, and the drip of red paint in the angel's lower lip and the saint's own rough hands ready to write the Gospel . . . ah miraculous too the veil of mistaken angel smoke on Tobias' departing angel's left arm.—— What can you do?

Suddenly I walked into the 19th Century room and there was an explosion of light —— of bright gold and daylight. Van Gogh, his crazy blue Chinese church with the hurrying woman, the secret of it the Japanese spontaneous brushstroke that, for instance, made the woman's back show, her back all white unpainted canvas except for a few black thick script strokes.—— Then the madness of blue running in the roof where Van Gogh had a ball —— I could see the joy red mad gladness he rioted in in that church heart.—— His maddest picture was gardens with insane trees whirling in the blue swirl sky, one tree finally exploding into just black lines, almost silly but divine —— the thick curls and butter burls of color, beautiful oil rusts, glubs, creams, greens.

I studied Dégas' ballet pictures —— how serious the perfect faces in the orchestra, then suddenly the explosion on the stage —— the pink film rose of the ballerina gowns, the puffs of color.—— And Cézanne, who painted exactly as he saw, more accurate and less divine than holy Van Gogh —— his green apples, his crazy blue lake with acrostics in it, his trick of hiding perspective (one jetty in the lake can do it, and one mountain line). Gauguin —— seeing him beside these masters, he seemed to me almost like a clever cartoonist.—— Compared to Renoir, too, whose painting of a French afternoon was so gorgeously colored with the Sunday afternoon of all our childhood dreams —— pinks, purples, reds, swings, dancers, tables, rosy cheeks and bubble laughter.

On the way out of the bright room, Frans Hals, the gayest of all painters who ever lived. Then one last look at Rembrandt's St. Matthew's angel —— its smeared red mouth *moved* when I looked.

APRIL IN Paris, sleet in Pigalle, and last moments. —— In my skidrow hotel it was cold and still sleeting so I put on my old blue jeans, old muffcap, railroad gloves and zip-up rain jacket, the same clothes I'd worn as a brakeman in the mountains of California and as a forester in the Northwest, and hurried across the Seine to Les Halles for a last supper of fresh bread and onion soup and *pâté*.—— Now for delights, walking in the cold dusk of Paris amid vast flower markets, then succumbing to thin crisp *frites* with rich sausage hot dog from a stall on the windswept corner, then into a mobbed mad restaurant full of gay workers and bourgeois where I was temporarily peeved because they forgot to bring me wine too, so gay and red in a clean stemmed glass. —— After eating, sauntering on home to pack for London tomorrow, then deciding to buy one final Parisian pastry, intending a Napoleon as usual, but because the girl thought I'd said "Milanais" I accepted her offer and took a bite of my Milanais as I crossed the bridge and bang! the absolutely final greatest of all pastries in the world, for the first time in my life I felt overpowered by a taste sensation, a rich brown mocha cream covered with slivered almonds and just a touch of cake but so pungent that it stole through my nose and taste buds like bourbon or rum with coffee and cream.—— I hurried back, bought another and had the second one with a little hot *espresso* in a café across the street from the Sarah Bernhardt Theater —— my last delight in Paris savoring the taste and watching Proustian showgoers coming out of the theater to hail cabs.

In the morning, at six, I rose and washed at the sink and the water running in my faucet talked in a kind of Cockney accent.—— I hurried out with full pack on back, and in the park a bird I never heard, a Paris warbler by the smoky morning Seine.

I took the train to Dieppe and off we went, through smoky suburbs, through Normandy, through gloomy fields of pure green, little stone cottages, some red brick, some half-timbered, some stone, in a drizzle along the canal-like Seine, colder and colder, through Vernon and little places with names like Vauvay and Something-sur-Cie, to gloomy Rouen, which is a horrible rainy dreary place to have been burned at the stake.—— All the time my mind excited with the thought of England by nightfall, London, the fog of real old London.—— As usual I was standing in the cold vestibule, no room inside the train, sitting occasionally on my pack crowded in with a gang of shouting Welsh schoolboys and their quiet coach who loaned me the *Daily Mail* to read.—— After Rouen the ever-more-gloomy Normandy hedgerows and meadows, then Dieppe with its red rooftops

and old quais and cobblestoned streets with bicyclists, the chimney pots smoking, gloom rain, bitter cold in April and I sick of France at last.

The channel boat crowded to the hilt, hundreds of students and scores of beautiful French and English girls with pony tails and short haircuts.—— Swiftly we left the French shore and after a spate of blank water we began to see green carpets and meadows stopped abruptly as with a pencil line at chalk cliffs, and it was that sceptered isle, England, springtime in England.

All the students sang in gay gangs and went through to their chartered London coach car but I was made to sit (I was a take-a-seater) because I had been silly enough to admit that I had only fifteen shillings equivalent in my pocket.—— I sat next to a West Indies Negro who had no passport at all and was carrying piles of strange old coats and pants —— he answered strangely the questions of the officers, looked extremely vague and in fact I remembered he had bumped into me absentmindedly in the boat on the way over.—— Two tall English bobbies in blue were watching him (and myself) suspiciously, with sinister Scotland Yard smiles and strange long-nosed brooding attentiveness like in old Sherlock Holmes movies.—— The Negro looked at them terrified. One of his coats dropped on the floor but he didn't bother to pick it up.—— A mad gleam had come into the eyes of the immigration officer (young intellectual fop) and now another mad gleam in some detective's eye and suddenly I realized the Negro and I were surrounded.—— Out came a huge jolly redheaded customs man to interrogate us.

I told them my story —— I was going to London to pick up a royalty check from an English publisher and then on to New York on the *Ile de France*.—— They didn't believe my story —— I wasn't shaved, I had a pack on my back, I looked like a bum.

"What do you *think* I am!" I said and the red-headed man said "That's just it, we don't quite know in the least what you were doing in Morocco, or in France, or arriving in England with fifteen bob." I told them to call my publishers or my agent in London. They called and got no answer — it was Saturday. The bobbies were watching me, stroking their chins.—— The Negro had been taken into the back by now — suddenly I heard a horrible moaning, as of a psychopath in a mental hospital, and I said "What's that?"

"That's your Negro friend."

"What's the matter with him?"

"He has no passport, no money, and is apparently escaped from a mental institution in France. Now do you have any way to verify this story of yours, otherwise we s'll have to detain you."

"In custody?"

"Quite. My dear fellow, you can't come into England with fifteen bob."

"My dear fellow, you can't put an American in jail."

"Oh yes we can, if we have grounds for suspicion."

"Dont you believe I'm a writer?"

"We have no way of knowing this."

"But I'm going to miss my train. It's due to leave any minute."

"My dear fellow . . ." I rifled through my bag and suddenly found a note in a magazine about me and Henry Miller as writers and showed it to the customs man. He beamed:

"Henry Miller? That's most unusual. We stopped *him* several years ago, he wrote quite a bit about New-haven." (This was a grimmer New Haven than the one in Connecticut with its dawn coalsmokes.) But the customs man was immensely pleased, checked my name again, in the article and on my papers, and said, "Well,

I'm afraid it's going to be all smiles and handshakes now. I'm awfully sorry. I think we can let you through —— with the provision that you leave England inside a month."

"Don't worry." As the Negro screamed and banged somewhere inside and I felt a horrible sorrow because he had not made it to the other shore, I ran to the train and made it barely in time.—— The gay students were all in the front somewhere and I had a whole car to myself, and off we went silently and fast in a fine English train across the countryside of olden Blake lambs. —— And I was safe.

English countryside —— quiet farms, cows, meads, moors, narrow roads and bicycling farmers waiting at crossings, and ahead, Saturday night in London.

Outskirts of the city in late afternoon like the old dream of sun rays through afternoon trees.—— Out at Victoria Station, where some of the students were met by limousines.—— Pack on back, excited, I started walking in the gathering dusk down Buckingham Palace Road seeing for the first time long deserted streets. (Paris is a woman but London is an independent man puffing his pipe in a pub).—— Past the Palace, down the Mall through St. James's Park, to the Strand, traffic and fumes and shabby English crowds going out to movies, Trafalgar Square, on to Fleet Street where there was less traffic and dimmer pubs and sad side alleys, almost clear to St. Paul's Cathedral where it got too Johnsonianly sad.—— So I turned back, tired, and went into the King Lud pub for a sixpenny Welsh rarebit and a stout.

I called my London agent on the phone, telling him my plight. "My dear fellow it's awfully unfortunate I wasnt in this afternoon. We were visiting mother in Yorkshire. Would a fiver help you?"

"Yes!" So I took a bus to his smart flat at Buckingham Gate (I had walked right past it after getting off the train) and went up to meet the dignified old couple.—— He with goatee and fireplace and Scotch to offer me, telling me about his one-hundred-year-old mother reading all of Trevelyan's *English Social History*.—— Homburg, gloves, umbrella, all on the table, attesting to his way of living, and myself feeling like an American hero in an old movie.—— Far cry from the little kid under a river bridge dreaming of England.—— They fed me sandwiches, gave me money, and then I walked around London savoring the fog in Chelsea, the bobbies wandering in the milky mist, thinking, "Who will strangle the bobby in the fog?" The dim lights, the English soldier strolling with one arm around his girl and with the other hand eating fish and chips, the honk of cabs and buses, Piccadilly at midnight and a bunch of Teddy Boys asking me if I knew Gerry Mulligan.—— Finally I got a fifteen-bob room in the Mapleton Hotel (in the attic) and had a long divine sleep with the window open, in the morning the carillons blowing all of an hour round eleven and the maid bringing in a tray of toast, butter, marmalade, hot milk and a pot of coffee as I lay there amazed.

And on Good Friday afternoon a heavenly performance of the *St. Matthew Passion* by the St. Paul's choir, with full orchestra and a special service choir.—— I cried most of the time and saw a vision of an angel in my mother's kitchen and longed to go home to sweet America again.—— And realized that it didn't matter that we sin, that my father died only of impatience, that all my own petty gripes didnt matter either.—— Holy Bach spoke to me and in front of me was a magnificent marble bas-relief showing Christ and three Roman soldiers listening: "And he spake unto them do violence to no man, nor accuse any falsely, and be content with thy wages." Outside as I walked in the dusk around Christopher Wren's great masterpiece and saw the gloomy overgrown ruins of Hitler's blitz around the cathedral, I saw my own mission.

In the British Museum I looked up my family in *Rivista Araldica*, IV, Page 240, "Lebris de Keroack. Canada, originally from Brittany. Blue on a stripe of gold with three silver nails. Motto: Love, work and suffer."

I could have known.

At the last moment I discovered the Old Vic while waiting for my boat train to Southampton.—— The performance was *Antony and Cleopatra*.—— It was a marvelously smooth and beautiful performance, Cleopatra's words and sobbings more beautiful than music, Enobarbus noble and strong, Lepidus wry and funny at the drunken rout on Pompey's boat, Pompey warlike and harsh, Antony virile, Caesar sinister, and though the cultured voices criticized the Cleopatra in the lobby at intermission, I knew that I had seen Shakespeare as it should be played.

On the train en route to Southampton, brain trees growing out of Shakespeare's fields, and the dreaming meadows full of lamb dots.

8. THE VANISHING AMERICAN HOBO

THE AMERICAN HOBO HAS A HARD TIME
hoboing nowadays due to the increase in police sur-
veillance of highways, railroad yards, sea shores, river
bottoms, embankments and the thousand-and-one hiding holes of industrial night.—— In California, the pack
rat, the original old type who goes walking from town
to town with supplies and bedding on his back, the
"Homeless Brother," has practically vanished, along
with the ancient gold-panning desert rat who used to
walk with hope in his heart through struggling Western towns that are now so prosperous they dont want
old bums any more.—— "Man dont want no pack rats
here even though they founded California" said an
old man hiding with a can of beans and an Indian fire
in a river bottom outside Riverside California in 1955.
—— Great sinister tax-paid police cars (1960 models
with humorless searchlights) are likely to bear down
at any moment on the hobo in his idealistic lope to

BATTERIES

Rivera

freedom and the hills of holy silence and holy privacy. —— There's nothing nobler than to put up with a few inconveniences like snakes and dust for the sake of absolute freedom.

I myself was a hobo but only of sorts, as you see, because I knew someday my literary efforts would be rewarded by social protection —— I was not a real hobo with no hope ever except that secret eternal hope you get sleeping in empty boxcars flying up the Salinas Valley in hot January sunshine full of Golden Eternity toward San Jose where mean-looking old bo's 'll look at you from surly lips and offer you something to eat and a drink too —— down by the tracks or in the Guadaloupe Creekbottom.

The original hobo dream was best expressed in a lovely little poem mentioned by Dwight Goddard in his *Buddhist Bible:*
Oh for this one rare occurrence
Gladly would I give ten thousand pieces of gold!
A hat is on my head, a bundle on my back,
And my staff, the refreshing breeze and the full moon.
In America there has always been (you will notice the peculiarly Whitmanesque tone of this poem, probably written by old Goddard) a definite special idea of footwalking freedom going back to the days of Jim Bridger and Johnny Appleseed and carried on today by a vanishing group of hardy old timers still seen sometimes waiting in a desert highway for a short bus ride into town for panhandling (or work) and grub, or wandering the Eastern part of the country hitting Salvation Armies and moving on from town to town and state to state toward the eventual doom of big-city skid rows when their feet give out.—— Nevertheless not long ago in California I did see (deep in the gorge by a railroad track outside San Jose buried in eucalyptus leaves and the blessed oblivion of vines) a bunch of cardboard and

jerrybuilt huts at evening in front of one of which sat an aged man puffing his 15¢ Granger tobacco in his corn-cob pipe (Japan's mountains are full of free huts and old men who cackle over root brews waiting for Supreme Enlightenment which is only obtainable through occasional complete solitude.)

In America camping is considered a healthy sport for Boy Scouts but a crime for mature men who have made it their vocation.—— Poverty is considered a virtue among the monks of civilized nations —— in America you spend a night in the calaboose if you're caught short without your vagrancy change (it was fifty cents last I heard of, Pard —— what now?)

In Brueghel's time children danced around the hobo, he wore huge and raggy clothes and always looked straight ahead indifferent to the children, and the families didnt mind the children playing with the hobo, it was a natural thing.—— But today mothers hold tight their children when the hobo passes through town because of what newspapers made the hobo to be —— the rapist, the strangler, child-eater.—— Stay away from strangers, they'll give you poison candy. Though the Brueghel hobo and the hobo today are the same, the children are different.—— Where is even the Chaplinesque hobo? The old Divine Comedy hobo? The hobo is Virgil, he leadeth.—— The hobo enters the child's world (like in the famous painting by Brueghel of a huge hobo solemnly passing through the washtub village being barked at and laughed at by children, St. Pied Piper) but today it's an adult world, it's not a child's world.—— Today the hobo's made to slink —— everybody's watching the cop heroes on TV.

Benjamin Franklin was like a hobo in Pennsylvania; he walked through Philly with three big rolls under his arms and a Massachussetts halfpenny on his hat.—— John Muir was a hobo who went off into the mountains with a pocketful of dried bread, which he soaked in creeks.

Did Whitman terrify the children of Louisiana when he walked the open road?

What about the Black Hobo? Moonshiner? Chicken snatcher? Remus? The black hobo in the South is the last of the Brueghel bums, children pay tribute and stand in awe making no comment. You see him coming out of the piney barren with an old unspeakable sack. Is he carrying coons? Is he carrying Br'er Rabbit? Nobody knows what he's carrying.

The Forty Niner, the ghost of the plains, Old Zacatecan Jack the Walking Saint, the prospector, the spirits and ghosts of hoboism are gone —— but they (the prospectors) wanted to fill their unspeakable sacks with gold.—— Teddy Roosevelt, political hobo —— Vachel Lindsay, troubadour hobo, seedy hobo —— how many pies for one of *his* poems? The hobo lives in a Disneyland, Pete-the-Tramp land, where everything is human lions, tin men, moondogs with rubber teeth, orange-and-purple paths, emerald castles in the distance looming, kind philosophers of witches.—— No witch ever cooked a hobo.—— The hobo has two watches you can't buy in Tiffany's, on one wrist the sun, on the other wrist the moon, both bands are made of sky.

> *Hark! Hark! The dogs do bark,*
> *The beggars are coming to town;*
> *Some in rags, some in tags,*
> *And some in velvet gowns.*

The Jet Age is crucifying the hobo because how can he hop a freight jet? Does Louella Parsons look kindly upon hobos, I wonder? Henry Miller would allow the hobos to swim in his swimming pool.—— What about Shirley Temple, to whom the hobo gave the Bluebird? Are the young Temples bluebirdless?

Today the hobo has to hide, he has fewer places to hide, the cops are looking for him, *calling all cars, calling all cars, hobos seen in the vicinity of Bird-in-Hand* —— Jean Valjean weighed with his sack of candelabra, screaming to youth, "There's your *sou,* your *sou!*" Beethoven was a hobo who knelt and listened to the light, a deaf hobo who could not hear other hobo complaints.—— Einstein the hobo with his ratty turtleneck sweater made of lamb, Bernard Baruch the disillusioned hobo sitting on a park bench with voice-catcher plastic in his ear waiting for John Henry, waiting for somebody very mad, waiting for the Persian epic.——

Sergei Esenin was a great hobo who took advantage of the Russian Revolution to rush around drinking potato juice in the backward villages of Russia (his most famous poem is called *Confessions of a Bum*) who said at the moment they were storming the Czar "Right now I feel like pissing through the window at the moon." It is the egoless hobo that will give birth to a child someday —— Li Po was a mighty hobo.—— ego is the greatest hobo —— Hail Hobo Ego! Whose monument someday will be a golden tin coffee can.

Jesus was a strange hobo who walked on water.——

Buddha was also a hobo who paid no attention to the other hobo.——

Chief Rain-In-The-Face, weirder even.——

W. C. Fields —— his red nose explained the meaning of the triple world, Great Vehicle, Lesser Vehicle, Diamond Vehicle.

THE HOBO IS BORN OF PRIDE, having nothing to do with a community but with himself and other hobos and maybe a dog.—— Hobos by the railroad embankments cook at night huge tin cans of coffee.—— Proud was the way the hobo walked through a town by the back doors where pies were cooling on window sills, the hobo was a mental leper, he didnt need to beg to eat, strong Western bony mothers knew his tinkling beard and tattered toga, *come and get it!* But proud be proud, still there was some annoyance because sometimes when she called *come and get it,* hordes of hobos came, ten or twenty at a time, and it was kind of hard to feed that many, sometimes hobos were inconsiderate, but not always, but when they were, they no longer held their pride, they became bums — they migrated to the Bowery in New York, to Scollay Square in Boston, to Pratt Street in Baltimore, to Madison Street in Chicago, to 12th Street in Kansas City, to Larimer Street in Denver, to South Main Street in Los Angeles, to downtown Third Street in San Francisco, to Skid Road in Seattle ("blighted areas" all) ——

The Bowery is the haven for hobos who came to the big city to make the big time by getting pushcarts and collecting cardboard.— Lots of Bowery bums are Scandinavian, lots of them bleed easily because they drink too much.— When winter comes bums drink a drink called smoke, it consists of wood alcohol and a drop of iodine and a scab of lemon, this they gulp down and wham! they hibernate all winter so as not to catch cold, because they dont live anywhere, and it gets very cold outside in the city in winter.— Sometimes hobos sleep arm-in-arm to keep warm, right on the sidewalk. Bowery Mission veterans say that the beer-drinking bums are the most belligerent of the lot.

Fred Bunz is the great Howard Johnson's of the bums — it is located on 277 Bowery in New York. They write the menu in soap on the windows.— You see the bums reluctantly paying fifteen cents for pig brains, twenty-five cents for goulash, and shuffling out in thin cotton shirts in the cold November night to go and make the lunar Bowery with a smash of broken bottle in an alley where they stand against a wall like naughty boys.—— Some of them wear adventurous rainy hats picked up by the track in Hugo Colorado or blasted shoes kicked off by Indians in the dumps of Juarez, or coats from the lugubrious salon of the seal and fish.—— Bum hotels are white and tiled and seem as though they were upright johns.—— Used to be bums told tourists that they once were successful doctors, now they tell tourists they were once guides for movie stars or directors in Africa and that when TV came into being they lost their safari rights.

In Holland they dont allow bums, the same maybe in Copenhagen. But in Paris you can be a bum —— in Paris bums are treated with great respect and are rarely refused a few francs.—— There are various kinds of classes of bums in Paris, the high-class bum has a dog and a baby carriage in which he keeps all his belongings, and that usually consists of old *France Soirs*, rags, tin cans, empty bottles, broken dolls.—— This bum sometimes has a mistress who follows him and his dog and carriage around.—— The lower bums dont own a thing, they just sit on the banks of the Seine picking their nose at the Eiffel Tower.——

The bums in England have English accents, and it makes them seem strange —— they don't understand bums in Germany.—— America is the motherland of bumdom.——

American hobo Lou Jenkins from Allentown Pennsylvania was interviewed at Fred Bunz's on The Bowery. —— "What you wanta know all this info for, what you want?"

"I understand that you've been a hobo travelin' around the country."

"How about givin' a fella few bits for some wine before we talk."

"Al, go get the wine."

"Where's this gonna be in, the *Daily News?*"

"No, in a book."

"What are you young kids doing here, I mean where's the drink?"

"Al's gone to the liquor store —— You wanted Thunderbird, wasnt it?"

"Yair."

Lou Jenkins then grew worse —— "How about a few bits for a flop tonight?"

"Okay, we just wanta ask you a few questions like why did you leave Allentown?"

"My wife.—— My wife, —— Never get married. You'll never live it down. You mean to say it's gonna be in a book hey what I'm sayin'?"

"Come on say something about bums or something.——"

"Well whattaya wanta know about bums? Lot of 'em around, kinda tough these days, no money —— lissen, how about a good meal?"

"See you in the Sagamore." (Respectable bums' cafeteria at Third and Cooper Union.)

"Okay kid, thanks a lot." —— He opens the Thunderbird bottle with one expert flip of the plastic seal. —— Glub, as the moon rises resplendent as a rose he swallows with big ugly lips thirsty to gulp the throat down, Sclup! and down goes the drink and his eyes be-pop themselves and he licks tongue on top lip and says "H-a-h!" And he shouts "Dont forget my name is spelled Jenkins, J-e-n-k-y-n-s.——"

Another character —— "You say that your name is Ephram Freece of Pawling New York?"

"Well, no, my name is James Russell Hubbard."

"You look pretty respectable for a bum."

"My grandfather was a Kentucky colonel."

"Oh?"

"Yes."

"Whatever made you come here to Third Avenue?"

"I really cant do it, I dont care, I cant be bothered, I feel nothing, I dont care any more. I'm sorry but—somebody stole my razor blade last night, if you can lay some money on me I'll buy myself a Schick razor."

"Where will you plug it in? Do you have such facilities?"

"A Schick injector."

"Oh."

"And I always carry this book with me —— *The Rules of St. Benedict*. A dreary book, but well I got another book in my pack. A dreary book too I guess."

"Why do you read it then?"

"Because I found it —— I found it in Bristol last year."

"What are you interested in? You like interested in something?"

"Well, this other book I got there is er, yee, er, a big strange book —— you shouldnt be interviewing me. Talk to that old nigra fella over there with the harmonica —— I'm no good for nothing, all I want is to be left alone ——"

"I see you smoke a pipe."

"Yeah —— Granger tobacco. Want some?"

"Will you show me the book?"

"No I aint got it with me, I only got this with me."
—— He points to his pipe and tobacco.

"Can you say something?"

"Lightin flash."

The American Hobo is on the way out as long as sheriffs operate with as Louis-Ferdinand Céline said, "One line of crime and nine of boredom," because having nothing to do in the middle of the night with everybody gone to sleep they pick on the first human being

180

they see walking.—— They pick on lovers on the beach even. They just dont know what to do with themselves in those five-thousand-dollar police cars with the two-way Dick Tracy radios except pick on anything that moves in the night and in the daytime on anything that seems to be moving independently of gasoline, power, Army or police.—— I myself was a hobo but I had to give it up around 1956 because of increasing television stories about the abominableness of strangers with packs passing through by themselves independently —— I was surrounded by three squad cars in Tucson Arizona at 2 A.M. as I was walking pack-on-back for a night's sweet sleep in the red moon desert:

"Where you goin'?"

"Sleep."

"Sleep where?"

"On the sand."

"Why?"

"Got my sleeping bag."

"Why?"

"Studyin' the great outdoors."

"Who are you? Let's see your identification."

"I just spent a summer with the Forest Service."

"Did you get paid?"

"Yeah."

"Then why dont you go to a hotel?"

"I like it better outdoors and it's free."

"Why?"

"Because I'm studying hobo."

"What's so good about that?"

They wanted an *explanation* for my hoboing and came close to hauling me in but I was sincere with them and they ended up scratching their heads and saying "Go ahead if that's what you want."—— They didnt offer me a ride four miles out to the desert.

And the sheriff of Cochise allowed me to sleep on the cold clay outside Bowie Arizona only because he didnt know about it.—— There's something strange going on, you cant even be alone any more in the primitive wilderness ("primitive areas" so-called), there's always a helicopter comes and snoops around, you need camouflage.—— Then they begin to demand that you observe strange aircraft for Civil Defense as though you knew the difference between regular strange aircraft and any kind of strange aircraft.—— As far as I'm concerned the only thing to do is sit in a room and get drunk and give up your hoboing and your camping ambitions because there aint a sheriff or fire warden in any of the new fifty states who will let you cook a little meal over some burning sticks in the tule brake or the hidden valley or anyplace any more because he has nothing to do but pick on what he sees out there on the landscape moving independently of the gasoline power army police station.—— I have no ax to grind: I'm simply going to another world.

Ray Rademacher, a fellow staying at the Mission in the Bowery, said recently, "I wish things was like they was when my father was known as Johnny the Walker of the White Mountains.—— He once straightened out a young boy's bones after an accident, for a meal, and left. The French people around there called him '*Le Passant.*' " (He who passes through.)

The hobos of America who can still travel in a healthy way are still in good shape, they can go hide in cemeteries and drink wine under cemetery groves of trees and micturate and sleep on cardboards and smash bottles on the tombstones and not care and not be scared of the dead but serious and humorous in the cop-avoiding night and even amused and leave litters of their picnic between the grizzled slabs of Imagined Death, cussing what they think are real days, but Oh the poor bum of the skid row! There he sleeps in the doorway, back to wall, head down, with his right hand palm-up as if to receive from the night, the other hand hanging, strong, firm, like Joe Louis hands, pathetic, made tragic by unavoidable circumstance —— the hand like a beggar's upheld with the fingers forming a suggestion of what he deserves and desires to receive, shaping the alms, thumb almost touching finger tips, as though on the tip of the tongue he's about to say in sleep and with that gesture what he couldnt say awake: "Why have you taken this away from me, that I cant draw my breath in the peace and sweetness of my own bed but here in these dull and nameless rags on this humbling stoop I have to sit waiting for the wheels of the city to roll," and further, "I dont want to show my hand but in sleep I'm helpless to straighten it, yet take this opportunity to see my plea, I'm alone, I'm sick, I'm dying —— see my hand up-tipped, learn the secret of my human heart, give me the thing, give me your hand, take me to the emerald mountains beyond the city, take me to the safe place, be kind, be nice, smile —— I'm too tired now of everything else, I've had enough, I give up, I quit, I want to go home, take me home O brother in the night —— take me home, lock me in safe, take me to where all is peace and amity, to the family of life, my mother, my father, my sister, my wife and you my brother and you my friend —— but no hope, no hope, no hope, I wake up and I'd give a million dollars to be in my own bed —— O Lord save me ——" In evil roads behind gas tanks where murderous dogs snarl from behind wire fences cruisers suddenly leap out like getaway cars but from a crime more secret, more baneful than words can tell.

The woods are full of wardens.